Dorothy Howell

BACKPACKS AND BETRAYALS

By

Dorothy Howell

Dorothy Howell

ISBN 978-0-9856930-8-4

Published in the United States of America

BACKPACKS AND BETRAYALS

Dorothy Howell

With love to Stacy, Judy, Brian, and Seth

The author is extremely grateful for the love, support, and help of many people. Some of them are: Stacy Howell, Judith Branstetter, Brian Branstetter, Seth Branstetter, Martha Cooper, Evie Cook, Rich Hayden, William F. Wu, Ph.D., and the talented people at Web Crafters Design.

MYSTERIES BY DOROTHY HOWELL

The Haley Randolph Mystery Series

Handbags and Homicide
Purses and Poison
Shoulder Bags and Shootings
Clutches and Curses
Tote Bags and Toe Tags
Evening Bags and Executions
Beach Bags and Burglaries
Swag Bags and Swindlers
Slay Bells and Satchels
Duffel Bags and Drownings
Fanny Packs and Foul Play
Pocketbooks and Pistols
Backpacks and Betrayals

The Dana Mackenzie Mystery Series

Fatal Debt
Fatal Luck
Fatal Choice

BACKPACKS AND BETRAYALS

By

Dorothy Howell

Dorothy Howell

Chapter 1

You never know when something good is going to happen to you—that's what I always say. Or maybe somebody else said it. Or I heard it somewhere—on TV, maybe, or I read it on the internet. I don't know. I can't remember.

Anyway, something totally fantastic happened and I, Haley Randolph, with my brunettes-look-smart hair and my five-foot-nine-is-really-tall-for-a-girl height, had jumped on the opportunity. Okay, really, I hadn't simply jumped. I'd actually hurled myself out of my chair, waved both arms in the air, and shouted, "I'll do it!" before anyone else in the meeting even realized what was going on.

This was, of course, in direction violation of my personal don't-volunteer-for-anything policy that had served me well through … actually, my entire 25 years of life. I prided myself on my commitment to adhering to this policy.

But I also prided myself on my flexibility. So when Priscilla, the office manager at L.A. Affairs where I worked as an event planner, had announced that the North Hollywood—more affectionately known as NoHo—Arts District's fashion crawl was our newest client, I knew this was something way good that I had to claim for myself.

So here I was walking down Lankershim Boulevard in North Hollywood on a brilliantly beautiful Southern California day—looking somewhat brilliantly beautiful myself in my black Donna Karan business suit which I'd accessorized with an awesome Chanel tote—heading for the KGE Model Agency, the fashion crawl's major sponsor.

The NoHo Arts District was home to an über-eclectic mix of theaters, art galleries, restaurants and shops, an urban mix of all things artistic. It wasn't unusual to spot a group of actors running lines, dancers practicing their moves, or musicians rehearsing a song—all of which seemed kind of out-there to me, but who was I to judge? Most people have some weirdness about them.

I mean that in the nicest way, of course.

—

3

Scattered among the artsy locations along Lankershim Boulevard and the adjoining streets were office buildings, banks, and a smattering of stores and shops for normal folks. Traffic was brisk, the sidewalks well-traveled with people dressed in everything from edgy bohemian to classic business suits.

The KGE Model Agency was located on the second floor of a two-story contemporary glass and concrete structure that had just undergone a major renovation. Many of the tenants had vacated the building and new ones were slowly moving in, leaving much of the office space currently unoccupied.

KGE billed itself as a full service agency that booked models for runway, print, and fittings. I'd been here many times talking with Peri, the office manager, about the fashion crawl. I'd worked at L.A. Affairs for a while now and had staged a lot of events, many of them for Hollywood insiders, stars, and celebrities, so I'd dealt with my share of problem clients. Luckily, Peri wasn't one of them—so far, anyway; the crawl was coming up soon, so anything could happen.

Since it was well past the usual lunch hour, the building's lobby was pretty quiet when I walked inside. Set around the large, contemporary, jeez-this-place-looks-totally-uninviting space were seating groups, a couple of fountains, and some maybe-these-will-warm-up-the-place planters teeming with greenery which looked to me like it was fake.

A uniformed security guard stood behind a granite counter in front of a bank of elevators. He was an old guy, probably in his fifties, so I didn't know how much actual security he could provide. I figured that, at best, he would be a credible witness if something went down.

A wide staircase on the left side of the lobby swept up to the second floor. Whoever had designed the building must have been some sort of fitness freak because there were stairs at both ends of the building and at the mid-point—and not the narrow kind meant for use only during an emergency. These were grand, mosaic and marble curving staircases that almost demanded to be used.

Obviously, the architect who'd come up with this oh-so-brilliant idea was a man who'd never spent a day in three-inch pumps.

For some odd reason, I always saw steps in public places as something of a personal challenge—not that I'm competitive, or anything, but at the gym I often find myself racing the stranger next to me on the stationary bike—so I ignored the elevators and headed up the stairs.

My mom was a former beauty pageant queen. Really. The one gene I'd inherited from her—not her stunning beauty; I was merely pretty, according to the whispers of everyone who'd ever laid eyes on the two of us—was the ability to walk well in stilettos. I trotted up the steps with what Mom would describe as displaying the ease and grace of Scarlet on the staircase at Twelve Oaks, and headed down the long hallway that ran through the middle of the building.

Office suites were on both sides, and some of them were fronted by smoked glass walls which put every reception and lobby area on display as if inside a fishbowl. This, of course, forced the receptionists to actually work. They couldn't sluff off and internet shop, or post on Facebook, or even book a pedi without every passerby peering inside, seeing their every move.

No way could I work under those conditions

Halfway down the corridor I pushed open the door to KGE. Their lobby walls were covered with framed photos of the models they represented, beautiful men and women with perfectly sculpted faces and bodies striking a variety of this-looks-sexy poses. KGE's logo—the company's letters entwined in neon yellow and run through with a purple lightning bolt—was mounted on the wall behind the reception desk.

I guessed the bolt of electricity was meant to demonstrate the power of the agency, but to me it said that landing a job as a model was as rare as being struck by lightning.

Three young women who'd made the cut were seated in the small lobby. I knew they were KGE models because they carried black backpacks with the agency's logo on the front, and because, even though they were a variety of sizes, shapes, and colors—including a plus-size—they were all blindingly gorgeous.

Misty—I think she made up her own name—was the receptionist. She sat behind a high counter studying her fingernails. I figured she was maybe 19, a size two, and had shoulder length blonde hair with pink tips. Misty was dressed to the max, obviously totally on board with the heightened fashion awareness expected from anyone who worked at this kind of agency.

—

5

I glanced down the hallway beside the reception desk where the private offices and conference rooms were located. I'd made an appointment with Peri this morning before I left L.A. Affairs. She was crazy punctual so I expected to spot her coming to the lobby to meet me, but I didn't see her.

I waited a couple of minutes, and just as I was seriously considering asking Misty to let Peri know I'd arrived—and maybe get a look at her nails, which she seemed totally fascinated with—the door swung open and Peri walked into the lobby from the hallway.

Peri had a definite office-manager vibe to her. I figured her for a year or so older than me. She had short brown hair cut in a chic style and, apparently, had ice water flowing through her veins since I'd never seen her even slightly rattled over anything that went down.

Today she was dressed in a fabulous gray YSL suit. Immediately, I mentally paired her outfit with a black Gucci clutch. The vision just popped into my head. Somehow, I'd developed the ability to instantly match the perfect bag to any outfit—sort of like a superpower.

I had a thing for designer handbags. To say I was simply crazy about them would do my obsession a disservice. My best friend Marcie Hanover was equally enthralled, which was one of the reasons we'd been BFFs forever.

"Hi, Haley," Peri said. "Have you been waiting long?"

"Just got here," I said, then forced some enthusiasm into my voice and asked, "Is Katrina here?"

I don't like Katrina.

"No, thank God," Peri said.

Nobody likes Katrina.

"Come on back," she said.

We walked down the hallway into Peri's office, a contemporary space with a floor-to-ceiling glass wall that overlooked Lankershim Boulevard. KGE definitely had a prime location in the building.

Peri dropped into the chair behind her neat, organized desk. I took a seat on the other side.

"How's it going? Any problems?" she asked, squaring off a stack of papers and laying them aside.

"Everything is on schedule," I told her as I pulled the L.A.

Affairs portfolio that I used to keep track of the event details out of my tote bag.

The KGE agency was the major sponsor and the founding force behind the NoHo fashion crawl, an event that was the brainchild of Katrina Granger, the owner.

Everyone referred to her as Hurricane Katrina.

Not to her face, of course.

I'd met Katrina during my initial planning meeting for the crawl and—yikes!—she was somewhere between awful and run-while-you-still-can.

Obviously, someone had fed her after midnight.

Katrina had turned everything over to Peri, thankfully, and we'd hit it off big-time. Peri had been a dream to work with, and despite Katrina's occasional interference, the event was coming together easily.

Hundreds of visitors were expected for the crawl and would be treated to everything that screamed fashion. A number of pop-up showrooms would feature upcoming clothing lines from many of the major designers. Fashion preview shows were scheduled throughout the event.

Kiosks would offer eyewear, jewelry, and accessories. A beauty bar would promote skin care, makeup, fragrance, and the latest in tools for waxing and facials. New trends in hair design would be presented. Fashion experts would appear on panels to discuss a number of topics.

This would be the first fashion crawl staged in NoHo. Everything had to be perfect. A ton of money had been invested. Reputations—and future events—were on the line.

Peri lifted a folder from the corner of her desk and presented it to me. "Here's the addendum."

The crawl was huge so the responsibilities had been divvied up between the sponsors. I was handling everything KGE had committed to—the agency's model showroom and recruitment center, the food and dessert stations, and the all-important VIP after-party.

KGE had decided to add the dessert stations after the original contract with L.A. Affairs had been negotiated. Our legal department usually handled all the details but since this was a last minute change, I'd offered to pick up the signed addendum to speed things along. L.A. Affairs wouldn't proceed with anything

—

without the original written authorization.

"Great," I said, tucking the folder into my tote bag.

We discussed the caterer's suggestions for the after-party. I wasn't crazy about some of the recommendations and neither was Peri so we came up with some ideas of our own—one of the reasons I liked doing event planning face-to-face.

"I'll run it by Katrina and get back with you," Peri promised.

"And I'll email you the info on the dessert stations as soon as I get it," I said. "The caterer is anxious to get started."

We left her office and headed down the hallway, then both of us slowed when we heard voices in the lobby—well, just one voice, really.

Hurricane Katrina had blown in.

Since there was no means of escape, I braced myself and followed Peri into the lobby.

Two of the three models I'd seen earlier were on their feet holding their KGE backpacks in front of them like body armor. Misty stood ramrod straight behind the reception desk looking like she was preparing to make a hostage video. Katrina had planted herself in the center of the lobby.

"We're all accountable," she announced, giving major stink-eye and swinging both arms around. "Each and every one of you. You're accountable."

Katrina was a full-figured gal, tall, with jet black hair. Her modeling days—if she'd ever had them—were well behind her. I figured her for fifty, easily. Yet that didn't stop her from dressing as if she were a twenty-year-old runway waif. Her style was— well, jeez, I didn't know what kind of style she was going for.

Today, as usual, she had full-on makeup complete with metallic eyeshadows. She wore a burgundy sweater with leather armholes, a denim maxi skirt, and red boots generously embellished with rhinestones. She didn't exactly pull it off but, of course, nobody was going to tell her.

"No exceptions. Everyone is accountable," Katrina declared, her gaze sweeping the room like a malfunctioning Terminator. She wagged her finger at me. "Even *this girl*."

I was the driving force behind the success for her fashion crawl and she hadn't bothered to remember my name. Nice, huh?

Since Peri and I had walked in during the middle of Katrina's tirade, I had no idea what everyone—including me, apparently—

was supposed to be accountable for, nor did I care.

This was one of the things I liked about my job: I could leave most any place, most any time I wanted.

"From now on—"

Katrina froze and swept the lobby once more.

"Where is Libby?" she demanded. "Libby? Libby?"

She called Libby's name as if she were hiding under a chair—which nobody would blame her for, of course—and would now come crawling out.

Libby had the unenviable job of being Katrina's personal assistant. I'd dealt with Libby a few times since the planning for the fashion crawl began. She was completely devoted to Katrina, which I didn't get.

Katrina drilled everyone in the room with her laser glare, as if one of us knew where Libby was and simply refused to tell her. Luckily, we were all saved when Libby appeared through the smoked glass wall, rushing through the hallway. She burst into the KGE office looking a little more harried than usual.

"I'm late. I'm late. I know I'm late," she declared, breathing heavily and looking up at Katrina as if her life depended on hearing that she wasn't in trouble.

I figured Libby for maybe 24 years old. She was petite, blonde, and pretty, and always dressed as fashionably as her surely meager PA salary allowed. Today she wore a navy blue business suit, a blouse with a bow at the throat, and sensible pumps.

She looked like she'd borrowed the outfit from her mom for a job interview.

"I dropped off your dry cleaning and went by the bank, like you wanted," Libby said, still huffing and puffing. "I got your car washed and delivered those papers. Everything's done. All of it. Just like you wanted."

Katrina continued to glare at Libby, but no way was I hanging around waiting for her to unthaw.

"I'll call you later," I whispered to Peri.

She looked slightly envious when I walked away.

In the hallway I breathed a sigh of relief, glad to be out of there. The rest of my afternoon was ahead of me and I had a few things that required my attention, but nothing pressing.

So what the heck? I decided. Why not do a little shopping

before heading back to the L.A. Affairs office?

Even though I'd been to North Hollywood a number of times, I'd never really looked at all the shops in the neighborhood. I decided to hit the restroom, then check out the NoHo stores and see what I could find because, as I always say, you never know when something good is going to happen to you.

As I headed down the corridor toward the restrooms at the rear of the building, I spotted a handbag lying at the top of the wide mid-point staircase that led down to the first floor.

Okay, that was weird.

I walked over and took a closer look.

Immediately, I recognized it as a non-designer, black shoulder bag. The faux-leather was creased and the handle slightly frayed.

It couldn't have been lying there long—I mean, jeez, how long did it take to realize you didn't have your handbag with you? I looked around for the person who must have dropped it. I didn't spot anyone. The hallway was empty. The glass-fronted office adjacent to the staircase was vacant.

I decided the best thing to do was take it to the old guy who worked at the security desk. He could hold it in lost-and-found, or maybe peek inside for some kind of ID.

When I bent down to pick it up I spotted a black flat lying on one of the steps.

Somebody had run out of her shoe *and* dropped her handbag?

I got a weird feeling.

I walked down to where the shoe lay.

My weird feeling got weirder.

I continued down and around the curve of the staircase. At the bottom, sprawled across the bottom steps and the floor, was a girl.

Oh, crap.

She was dead.

Chapter 2

I rushed down the staircase and stood in the hallway staring down at the dead girl. She looked young, probably no older than me. She had long dark hair and was dressed in black jeans and a tunic; a cell phone lay just beyond her outstretched arm. At first glance she appeared to be sleeping, except for the unnatural way her neck was bent, and the blood that trickled from her nose.

"What happened?" a voice behind me demanded.

I glanced back and saw a guy striding toward me from the rear of the building. He had on white painter's pants over a white T-shirt—both splattered with a rainbow of paint splotches—and was wiping his hands on a rag. His blond hair touched his collar and his bangs were plastered to his sweaty forehead.

He stopped beside me and stared at the girl.

"Call 9-1-1," he told me, a this-is-an-emergency command in his voice. He patted his pockets. "I haven't got my phone on me—"

"She's dead," I said.

He looked hard at me, then at the girl, and back at me again.

"You don't know that," he insisted. "Call—"

"Yes, I do," I said. "She's dead."

I had, unfortunately, seen my share of dead people, but I saw no reason to go into it with this guy.

"Stay here. Don't let anyone get near the crime scene," I said.

"Crime scene?" he asked, drawing back a little. "It was an accident. She fell down the stairs."

"Did you see her fall?" I asked.

"Well, no," he admitted, then glanced down at her again. "Maybe she was on her phone, not paying attention, and fell."

"I saw her handbag at the top of the stairs," I said. "She wouldn't have rolled all the way down here without help."

His eyes grew wider. "You think somebody pushed her? Deliberately?"

Even though I'd found myself in this situation before, that

didn't mean I wanted to hang around and have a discussion.

"I'll notify security."

I headed down the corridor toward the front of the building. In the lobby, about a half dozen people were coming and going, some taking the stairs, others waiting for the elevators. The guard was at his post behind the security desk.

"There's a dead girl back there," I told him, pointing.

His eyes popped open wider and his jaw sagged a little.

"You need to call 9-1-1," I said.

He seemed frozen in place for a few seconds, then whipped around and looked down the hallway.

"You should call right now," I said.

The guard snatched up the phone on his security console and started punching numbers.

I knew what would happen next—uniform cops would show up, followed by detectives, and the crime lab techs. I knew, too, they'd want to talk to me and would get around to it eventually.

No way was I hanging around all that time—not when a mere block away was one of my favorite locations on the entire planet.

I headed for the door.

"Hey, wait," the security guard called. "You can't leave!"

I left.

* * *

Aside from having lost my mind over designer handbags, I was also totally obsessed with Starbucks. I mean, really, how could I not be? What could be more comforting than a chilled blast of chocolate, sugar, and caffeine all in one beverage, the mocha frappuccino?

I took a seat at the window, sipped my frappie, and watched as, across the street, squad cars arrived at the building housing KGE, followed shortly by two detectives in a plain vanilla vehicle. I pretty much knew what would happen next and, honestly, I didn't want to think too much about it, so I decided to distract myself by texting Marcie—which was exactly what a BFF was for.

We'd both been on the hunt to identify the latest hottest-bag-of-the-season but hadn't found anything yet. Maybe she'd seen a fabulous tote or satchel I could check out online, and give my day the boost it desperately needed.

Just as I grabbed my cell phone from my tote, it buzzed. Mom's name appeared on the caller ID screen.

In addition to my don't-volunteer-for-anything policy, I also had a don't-answer-when-Mom-calls policy. Mom didn't know about my policy—it never occurred to her that anyone would not answer when she called—so really, it wasn't hurting anyone.

Being a former beauty queen who'd never abdicated her throne, Mom's life tended to revolve around herself, pageants, herself, fashion, herself, beauty, herself—and, well, there's only so much of that I can take.

Yet things promised to get worse very soon.

My cousin on Mom's side of the family—certainly not Dad's side, whom Mom referred to as the Clampetts—was getting married in a lavish extravaganza at the Four Seasons in Beverly Hills, and our entire family was attending.

An event of this magnitude, with its inevitable whose-child-turned-out-smarter-thinner-richer-better-looking one-upsmanship, was something I preferred to avoid at all costs. The comparison to my sister—a model and UCLA student—and my brother—a fighter pilot in the Air Force—left me woefully lacking, not to mention, of course, how I stacked up against my cousins.

Never had a family gathering taken place that I didn't find myself on the receiving end of several you-lost-that-job-too eyebrow bobs, whatever-happened-to-that-last-guy-you-were-dating questions, and a number of you-still-don't-have-a-career-path eye-rolls. True, it had taken me longer than most everyone else in the family to settle-in—career-wise, at least—and while my L.A. Affairs job was totally awesome, I wasn't looking forward to enduring all those questions and remarks.

I stared at Mom's name on the caller ID screen for a few more seconds. Since I was stuck here at Starbucks for a while and needed to fill my time somehow, I decided to get it over with—sort of like ripping off a bandage, although *that* would be more pleasurable.

"You're not going to believe what your cousin is doing," Mom declared when I answered.

I didn't bother to respond. Mom would tell me. She was a world-class gossip—along with most everyone else on her side of the family. Really, it was their sport. If it were an Olympic

---

event, they would have the Gold.

"She's thinking of changing the menu and serving Ethiopian food at the reception." Mom made a decidedly unpageantlike noise. "I can't imagine what she's thinking."

I hoped that didn't mean the bride had also decided to cancel the open bar.

Really, every family event needed an open bar.

"Oh, and here's some exciting news," Mom declared. "Your sister will be living in Paris for several months."

My sister—my younger sister who'd inherited Mom's stunning beauty—was moving to Paris? *Paris?*

"She'll be the muse for one of the most celebrated new fashion designers in the world," Mom told me. "I can't wait to tell everyone at the wedding. Isn't that fabulous news?"

Yeah, okay, it was great for my sister and I was happy for her. All our relatives and friends at the wedding would surely be impressed—maybe so much so that none of them would think to ask what I was doing with my life.

I could only hope.

"Got to run," Mom said, and we ended the call.

I dropped my phone into my tote bag. A number of things needed my attention this afternoon and I had to get them handled, which meant there was nothing left to do but go talk to the homicide detectives.

I grabbed my frappie and left.

* * *

The building was on lock-down. The double glass doors were propped open and two uniformed officers were turning away everyone who approached. Gazing past them into the building, I spotted crime scene tape stretched across the hallway and about a half-dozen official-looking men and women scurrying around.

In the lobby, I saw two men wearing off-the-rack suits that screamed I'm-a-homicide-detective. They were talking to the painter. The security guard was at his post apparently trying to look official by giving serious stink-eye to a group of lookey-loos gathered on the staircase.

As I approached the door, one of the officers held up his hand.

"I need to talk to the detectives," I explained. "I was here earlier and I—"

"That's her! That's her!" the security guard shouted. "She's the one!"

Everybody turned and stared. The detectives headed toward me. The two officers closed in.

Yikes! What the heck was going on?

My first instinct was to run but the vision of being thrown to the ground, handcuffed, and featured on every internet sign-in page courtesy of camera-happy bystanders stopped me.

"She's the one." The security guard barreled toward me, pointing. "She's the one who fled the scene."

The homicide detectives beat him to the door. They were both graying, slightly overweight, with been-there-done-that-way-too-many-times expressions.

The two detectives planted themselves in front of me. The uniformed officers circled around behind, hemming me in.

Not a great feeling.

"Miss, do you have knowledge of this incident?" one of the detectives asked.

"Yes," I said, trying for a what's-the-big-deal-I'm-innocent tone.

"Would you come inside?" the other detective asked.

They stepped back as I entered the lobby, then led the way to a spot in the corner. I caught sight of the painter standing nearby and did a double-take.

Oh my God, he was really good looking.

When I'd seen him in the hallway earlier I'd gotten the impression that he was kind of old, but now I saw that he was late-twenties, maybe thirty. Tall, with muscles bulging under the short sleeves of his paint-splattered T-shirt.

Jeez, why hadn't I noticed that before?

Maybe my thoughts had been clouded by the smell of paint and turpentine.

Or maybe it was the dead body.

I sensed everybody in the lobby staring as the detectives asked for my ID. I handed over my driver's license and they introduced themselves as Lindquist and Hoffman.

"Why did you leave the scene?" Detective Hoffman asked, as he copied my info into a little notepad.

"I went to Starbucks," I said, holding up my cup.

"Leaving makes you look guilty," Lindquist said.

"I came back," I pointed out.

They didn't seem to appreciate that fact.

"We have a witness who discovered the body," Hoffman said, handing back my ID.

Their witness, obviously, was the painter. I didn't have to be an LAPD detective to figure that out.

"You were seen coming down the staircase, standing over the victim," Lindquist told me.

I glanced at the painter. Oh my God, was he throwing me under the bus?

"You want to explain how that happened?" Hoffman asked, and his tone indicated there was no way I could possibly do that.

"I had nothing to do with this," I insisted.

Lindquist and Hoffman exchanged a look, then gave me major homicide detective stink-eye.

"Are you claiming you don't know the victim?" Hoffman asked.

"I have no idea who she is," I said.

The detectives shared a should-we-slap-on-the-cuffs look.

"Are you sure you want to stick with that story?" Lindquist asked. "We have a witness who told us you'd been involved with the victim."

Oh my God, what the heck were these guys talking about?

"So who was she?" I asked.

"She worked for the KGE Model Agency."

Oh, crap. This couldn't be good.

"You're involved with that agency," Detective Hoffman said. "Don't bother to deny it. We have a witness who confirmed you've been spending a great deal of time there lately."

It was the security guard, obviously, and he'd wasted no time pointing a finger at me.

"I'm an event planner. I'm working with KGE on the fashion crawl," I said, trying to make my connection to the agency sound minimal.

I mean, really, how much further could a fashion crawl be from a murder?

"So you *do* have a connection to the agency," Lindquist said. "*And* the victim."

Okay, so maybe the detectives had a point—not that I intended to agree with them.

"She didn't look familiar." I glanced down the hallway. "Who was she?"

Hoffman consulted his notepad and said, "Her name is Rayna Fuller. She's one of the agency's models."

The name didn't ring a bell. I hadn't interacted with any of the models but I'd seen them in the agency's lobby and had passed them in the hallways. Rayna was pretty—even dead, which says something about her—and full-figured, making her one of KGE's plus-size models.

"According to our witness," Hoffman said, "you immediately assumed this wasn't an accident, that the victim had been murdered. Why is that?"

I didn't like the way this conversation was going.

"Is that because you're the one who pushed her down the stairs?" Lindquist asked.

Okay, now I really didn't like where this was going.

"You were seen standing over her," Hoffman said. "It looks like you came down the stairs to make sure she was dead."

"Is that what happened?" Lindquist asked.

"Is it?" Hoffman echoed.

They both glared at me like they really expected me to confess. The security guard was staring, along with the painter and all the nosey Nellies gathered on the staircase.

No way was I hanging around to answer any more questions.

I channeled my mom's how-dare-you attitude and said, "I had nothing to do with this except to find the body. That's it. If you have any more questions, you know where to find me."

I whipped around and left the building.

I made it almost to the curb when I glanced back and saw somebody running toward me.

Chapter 3

"Hey, wait! Hold up!"

Shouting and hurrying toward me was the painter, the guy who'd ratted me out to the detectives and implicated me in Rayna Fuller's death. No way did I want to talk to him—except he was really good looking.

I stopped.

We've all got our priorities.

He gestured toward the building with his chin and said, "I saw those detectives giving you a hard time."

A couple of days' worth of whiskers darkened his jaw and—wow—he had really blue eyes. Still, I intended to blast him for trying to make me look guilty.

He must have read my expression because he said, "I didn't tell them you were involved in what happened. I just told them what I saw."

"Which was what?" I asked.

He shrugged. "That I was working, checking the hall every few minutes. The next time I looked, the girl was lying there and you were coming down the stairs."

Okay, that sounded innocent enough, and I knew homicide detectives had a way of twisting witness statements to try and get a confession.

"I just wanted you to know that I wasn't trying to make you look guilty, or anything," he said, sounding genuinely concerned.

I fumed for a few more seconds just to let him know none of this suited me, then said, "Thanks."

He grinned, and oh-yeah, he had a killer grin.

I couldn't help grinning back.

"Clark Phillips," he said, extending his hand.

We shook and a wave of warmth zinged up my arm as I introduced myself.

"So, do you work here?" he asked, nodding toward the building.

"I work for L.A. Affairs."

His brows bobbed, which was the reaction I often got from men when they heard the company's name and assumed it was a call girl service.

"We do event planning," I said.

He looked surprised and slightly disappointed—another reaction I usually got from men.

"And you're a painter," I said, waving my fingers at his paint-splattered clothing.

"Yeah, I guess you could call it that," he said. "I've been working in one of the offices at the rear of the building for the last couple of days."

Since he seemed willing to talk, I decided to see if I could find out anything more in case the homicide detectives wanted to question me again.

"Did you see anything unusual today?" I asked.

"Nothing," he said.

"Hear anything?" I asked. "Loud voices? Shouting, maybe? An argument?"

"It's pretty quiet back there. None of the offices are occupied." Clark paused for a few seconds then said, "You were right. That girl didn't fall accidentally. I heard the detective say her shirt was torn and there were scratches on her arm like she'd been grabbed and had struggled with somebody. They think she was pushed down the stairs."

Being right about a murder didn't exactly perk up my day.

He glanced at the building again. "I'd better get back to work. Maybe I'll see you again?"

"I'm involved with the fashion crawl so I'll definitely be around," I said.

He grinned. "Good."

After a few steps he turned back, his grin gone.

"I overheard the security guard talking to the detectives, trying to make something out of you being in the building so often," Clark said. "He claims you always used the staircase at the front of the building. He didn't know why you were on the one in the middle where the girl was murdered. The cops wondered the same thing."

Oh, crap.

* * *

"Something's going down," Bella told me.

We were standing in line inside the Holt's Department Store employee breakroom waiting for another three minutes of our lives to tick by so we could clock-in. Around us, other employees were heating meals in the microwave, munching on snacks from the vending machines, and wondering where it had all gone so wrong.

Or maybe that was just me.

After a full day at L.A. Affairs, I'd morphed into my much less cool persona of part-time sales clerk at Holt's, a seriously crappy midrange store. I'd taken the gig during my pre-L.A. Affairs days when I'd been desperate for money, then stayed because the company had purchased a chain of high-end boutiques that gave an astounding eighty-percent employee discount on designer clothing and accessories.

Call me shallow.

"We've got to go to a meeting," Bella said, nodding to the sign posted over the time clock.

Damn. Another butt-flattening, mind-numbing meeting.

"What now?" I murmured.

"It'll be some b.s.," Bella said.

"Something that will benefit management," I said.

"Yeah. Like I said, b.s."

I didn't disagree.

Bella, mocha to my vanilla, was tall, about my age, and worked at Holt's to save for beauty school. She intended to be a hairdresser to the stars, and practiced unique styles on herself. Tonight she'd sculpted her hair into what looked like a blooming flower atop her head.

The line moved forward. I punched in my employee number and pressed my fingertip to the scanner, and trailed behind everyone out of the breakroom.

The Holt's job had brought me not only a terrific employee discount at our sister store but an unexpected perk, my ex-official boyfriend, Ty Cameron, who ran the company that his family had owned for five generations. Ty was handsome, generous, kind, intelligent—there wasn't anything Ty couldn't do well, except be a decent boyfriend. His duties to Holt's came first. We'd broken up. I was putting maximum effort into not thinking about him.

It helped that I was kind-of seeing somebody else. Liam Douglas was an attorney. Our relationship was moving at a glacial pace, making it unlikely he'd achieve official-boyfriend status any time soon. It suited us both.

I moved along with the other employees down the hall, past the store managers' offices, and into the training room. The chairs were set up theater-style. I slipped into a seat on the back row behind the big guy who worked in menswear, my usual spot where I could drift off unnoticed if necessary.

Jeanette, the store manager, stood at the front of the room.

Yikes!

I turned away, hoping I hadn't sustained retina damage looking at her outfit.

Even though Jeanette was a full-figured gal and her best years were behind her—figuratively and literally—she could have still pulled off some awesome looks. But she insisted on dressing in Holt's dreadful so-called fashions. And as if that weren't bad enough, tonight she'd put her own spin on her outfit by dressing head-to-toe in leopard print. Pencil skirt, blouse, jacket, shoes, earrings, necklace, and bracelet—maybe even her underwear, too, only no way did I want to know for sure.

All the employees found seats and settled down. Jeanette started talking and I drifted off.

I mean, really, how could I not?

That thing at KGE today had been taking up a lot of space in my head—the murder, not that hot guy, Clark.

Well, okay, I was thinking about him, too.

But mostly I was thinking about the murder.

As Jeanette yammered on I thought back to this afternoon when I left the KGE office after my meeting with Peri, then witnessed Katrina's tirade over whatever it was everyone—including me—was accountable for, and had headed down the hallway toward the restroom. I hadn't seen anyone. I'd heard nothing, either.

When I'd discovered Rayna Fuller lying at the bottom of the staircase it hadn't occurred to me that she was connected to the KGE agency, even though she was plus size—meaning that by decree of some unseen but all knowing fashion gods she'd been deemed as such because her dress size was a double digit—and looked good, despite being dead.

—

I figured that some sort of confrontation had taken place at the head of the staircase. Clark had overheard the detectives say her shirt had been torn and there were scratches on her arm. Obviously, there'd been a scuffle.

Clark had been ducking in and out of the office he was painting, watching the hallway, when he'd spotted Rayna's body. She must have been pushed shortly before I spotted her, and she must have been pushed hard to have tumbled all the way down to the first floor.

Yuck. Not a great picture in my head.

Still, the image circled through my mind. Something didn't seem quite right about it but I couldn't put my finger on it.

Bella nudged me with her elbow, bringing me back to the moment, only marginally better than thoughts of a murder.

"Do you believe this?" she whispered and bobbed her brows toward Jeanette still blabbing at the front of the room.

I had no idea what she was talking about, of course, so I answered her eyebrow bob with an eye roll. She nodded wisely.

It hit me then that Rayna's murder must be connected to KGE—I don't know why but the thought popped into my head. That sort of thing just happened from time to time. But it made sense. Why else would Rayna have been in the building?

I flashed on my visit to the KGE office. I'd arrived on time. Peri had come in late, even though she was very punctual and knew I'd be there. When I'd finished my meeting and walked back to the lobby with Peri, one of the three models who'd been there earlier was gone. Misty was manning her post behind the reception desk. Libby, the beleaguered personal assistant, rushed in. Katrina was there, having just arrived.

My thoughts shot in a this-could-be-bad-for-me direction. I started to feel kind of panicky.

Oh my God, Katrina was there. Had the homicide detectives talked to her about Rayna's death? Had they let on that they suspected I was involved?

I went into semi-panic mode.

What if Katrina fired me? What if she raised such a stink that L.A. Affairs fired me, too?

For a few seconds—a very few seconds—I considered beating Katrina to the punch by telling the office manager at L.A. Affairs exactly what had happened, but I came to my senses. No way was I doing that.

Another of my personal policies was to never pass along unfavorable info unless it was absolutely necessary or benefited me in some way. This situation met neither of those criteria.

L.A. Affairs lived or died by its reputation. If they detected even the slightest hint that something was amiss, they might pull me off the fashion crawl. And worst still, the bad publicity might jeopardize the entire event—which could be seen as being my fault.

Yikes!

I absolutely couldn't lose my fabulous job at L.A. Affairs. Who would hire me again with that on my record? What would become of me? How would I live? I'd have no money except—

Oh my God. *Oh my God.*

I'd have to work at Holt's *forever.*

No way could I let that happen.

I was going to have to find Rayna's killer myself.

Just as a zillion ideas popped into my head, the big guy from menswear stood up. Everybody stood up.

Jeez, the meeting was over already?

Everybody chattered and seemed kind of happy, which was really odd after leaving a meeting. Even Bella looked stunned.

"Can you believe it?" she muttered, as we moved out of the training room and down the hallway.

Maybe I could, if I had any idea what had gone on in the meeting.

When we reached the sales floor, Sandy, my other BFF at Holt's, spotted us and rushed out of the women's clothing department holding the stack of everybody-shield-your-eyes T-shirts she'd been folding.

"You got the news? I heard all about it in the noon meeting," she said, smiling and bouncing on her toes.

Sandy was about my age with red or blonde hair, depending on her mood, that she most always wore in a ponytail. She'd worked at Holt's since before I'd come on board, although I didn't know why she stayed.

She could have done a lot better elsewhere. Really, Sandy could have done a lot better with a number of things, mainly her tattoo artist boyfriend who treated her like crap. I'd encouraged her to dump that idiot but, for some reason, she continued to ignore my oh-so-brilliant advice.

"Isn't it the coolest thing?" Sandy said, her ponytail bouncing.

"No, not really," Bella grumbled.

"Come on," Sandy insisted. "Contests are fun."

Holt's was having another contest for the employees? That's what the meeting had been about? Just as well I hadn't been listening.

"Some of us have done really well in the contests," Sandy pointed out, giving me a you-know-I'm-right look.

It was true that I'd scored pretty well on past contests but, well, let's just say it hadn't gone smoothly.

"Unless we get stuck with one of those beach towels again," Bella said.

We all groaned.

The Holt's beach towel—white with a huge blue cursive "H" in the center that served as the company's logo—was the go-to consolation prize for every contest. Apparently some genius in the marketing department had decided it was a good way to advertise the store, and it might have worked if they had thought the idea through completely.

Or they could have simply asked *me.*

Really, why wasn't I running the entire world?

"Well, yes," Sandy agreed. "The beach towels weren't the best quality."

"Mine started to fray the second time I washed it," Bella said. "The blue on that big "H" ran, then it fell apart before I'd used it a half dozen times."

"Still, a contest is fun," Sandy said. "And you might win one of the big prizes. They're pretty cool."

Judging by Bella's eye roll, I knew it was just as well that my thoughts had been elsewhere during the meeting. No way was I putting any effort into trying to win a Holt's contest. Plus, I didn't want to take a chance that I would end up with a Holt's beach towel because no way was I showing up at the beach or pool with that thing and have everybody think I actually shopped at a place like this. I was working here for the awesome discount at the Nuovo boutique—and that was prize enough for me.

"Have you seen the Holt's new spring fashion line yet?" Bella asked and shook her head.

I wondered if this was something else Jeanette had mentioned in the meeting and—yikes!—I was glad I hadn't been paying attention. Holt's clothing lines had nothing to do with fashion.

"It's under wraps in the stockroom," Sandy said.

"Yeah, and it should stay covered up," Bella said. "I looked at it—"

"Nobody is supposed to see it yet," Sandy insisted. "Not until the grand reveal when the contest winners are announced."

Before Bella could respond, Rita, the cashier's supervisor, walked up looking grumpy and cranky, as usual.

"You're not going to win anything in the contest standing around and talking," Rita barked. "Not that you'll win something, anyway."

She hates me.

"Especially you, princess," she said to me.

I hate her back.

Rita was dressed in her usual stretch pants and T-shirt with a farm animal on the front, this one featuring sheep embellished with orange glitter for no apparent reason.

"You're going to have to put in some effort, if you expect to qualify for anything," Rita said, giving me major stink-eye.

What the heck? Why was she giving me such a hard time?

"And not cause any problems," Rita said.

Well, okay, there'd been a few incidents in the past that involved me here at Holt's, but everything had turned out okay in the end ... kind of.

Besides, I didn't have time to think about a Holt's contest, or anything else at the store. I had to get going on my investigation and figure out who'd murdered Rayna before I lost my job at L.A. Affairs, and my life—the cool part of it, anyway—came to an end.

Chapter 4

I loved my office at L.A. Affairs. It was situated on the third floor of a high rise at the intersection of Sepulveda and Ventura in Sherman Oaks, one of L.A.'s many upscale areas. It was decorated in neutrals with splashes of blue and yellow, and featured a big window that overlooked the Galleria shopping center as well as an impressive number of office buildings, restaurants, and businesses.

The thing I liked most about my office was that it was private. This afforded me the opportunity to handle all my responsibilities without interruption—and it kept anyone wandering past from seeing exactly what I was doing.

When I got to the office the next morning I immediately jumped into my routine, which meant that I dropped off my handbag—a totally awesome Prada satchel which I'd paired with a gray business suit, accessorized with silver and white—and headed straight to the breakroom.

This was a crucial step in my day. I took more than the usual fifteen minutes required to prepare a single cup of coffee and listened for any indication that word had made it back to L.A. Affairs that a KGE model had been murdered. Luckily, nobody said anything. I hung out in the breakroom for another ten minutes just to be sure—and to eat a chocolate doughnut.

Just because the staff wasn't gossiping about it didn't mean management hadn't been informed. It was way too early in the day to relax completely. I'd have to stay on my toes and not draw attention to myself in any way.

My usual morning routine included updating my Facebook page, so that's the first thing I did when I settled into my office. I mean, really, was there a need to do actual work first thing in the morning when I might get fired at any moment?

I followed up my Facebook post by looking at my bank balance and booking a facial. My checking account was in good shape and I got the exact appointment time I'd requested, a sign that things were going my way. Then I got a text from Liam, my sort-of-kind-of boyfriend, saying he hoped my day was going well. Wow, was that nice, or what? I texted back an oh-so-clever response.

Just as I was thinking that nothing bad would happen, my cell phone buzzed. Mom's name appeared in the ID screen.

Crap.

An all too familiar wave of dread washed through me but I shook it off. So far, I'd experienced no problems today. Seemed I was on a roll. My mojo was working. I had to stay positive.

"There's news," Mom declared when I answered.

From her tone, I knew I was in for a pre-wedding update involving one of my cousins.

I braced myself.

"You remember your cousin who dropped out of college and went to live in some ridiculous artists' colony in Ecuador?" Mom asked.

My spirits lifted. Yes, I remembered her. She was one of the few family members who actually made me look good.

"I just found out that she's turned herself around," Mom said. "She graduated from medical school."

I slumped down in my chair.

"She's a pediatric cardiologist."

Why had I answered my phone?

Really, what's wrong me sometimes?

Mom blabbed on but I wasn't listening because a miniscule ray of hope suddenly beamed into my head.

Maybe I could get out of going to the wedding. After all the relatives heard about my sister's move to Paris and my cousin's altruistic career, would anyone even notice if I wasn't there?

"You know, Mom, I might not be able to—"

"I've got to call your sister with the news," Mom said and hung up.

Yeah, now my day definitely needed a boost.

Nobody here at the office had mentioned Rayna's death so I figured Katrina hadn't pulled me off the fashion crawl. Maybe the homicide detectives hadn't told Katrina that I'd found the body or that they were suspicious about my involvement. Maybe Katrina, if she'd been told and wanted me fired, had assigned the task of ratting me out to Libby, who'd been too overwhelmed to get to it yet. Maybe something else was going on—or maybe nothing was going on.

Either way, I couldn't sit around waiting and worrying that my life might be ripped apart at any moment. That's not how I roll.

I gathered my things and left the office.

* * *

I'd promised Peri I would email her the menu for the dessert stations as soon as I received it from the caterer, but I decided to deliver it in person instead. This would provide good cover for checking things out at KGE.

I parked my Honda in a lot on Magnolia Boulevard and headed for the building. Across the street, Starbucks called to me. Really. It's like there's a psychic connection, or something. But I'd called Peri on the drive over. She was expecting me and I didn't want to keep her waiting, so I kept walking.

I can make the hard decisions when I have to.

Besides, I could always get a frappie on my way out.

In the lobby, the old-guy security guard spotted me immediately, frowned, and reached for the phone on his console.

Oh my God. Had the homicide detectives told him to report my presence in the building? Was I under surveillance?

Not a great feeling.

I hurried up the stairs.

As I approached the KGE office I heard a voice drifting into the deserted hallway. Through the smoked glass panel, I spotted Katrina standing in the lobby.

My first instinct was to whip around and hide out in the ladies room until she left, and I would have done that but I spotted the security guard at the top of the staircase, eyeing me. Oh my God, he'd actually followed me.

Damn. Leaving now would make me look hugely suspicious. I pushed through the door.

Misty stood at attention behind her reception desk, and two models clutching their KGE backpacks sat up straight in their chairs. Katrina had planted herself in the middle of the lobby and was talking on her cell phone.

"Libby? Libby? Libby, where are you?" she said into her phone. "Where are you? Libby? Libby, which aisle are you on?"

Nobody in the lobby moved or spoke. Everyone stared like passersby at a train wreck.

"Libby? Libby, what are you seeing? Tell me what you're seeing."

Today Katrina had on what I could only think was a hippie retro style, recalling the you-call-that-fashion Haight-Ashbury look—elephant-leg jeans, a peasant blouse, and moccasins.

Really, if you're old enough to have worn it the first time around, it's best to stay away.

"Libby? Libby, are they the brown rice tortillas, or the corn tortillas?" Katrina asked. "Now look closely, Libby. Are they the handmade, or are they original?"

I wasn't sure why we'd all been subjected to Katrina's phone call but here we were, frozen in a Libby-goes-shopping tableau.

"Libby? Libby? Read the back, Libby. Look at the ingredients. Are you reading the ingredients, Libby?"

It was as if Katrina had her own gravitational pull that nobody could escape.

"And they're gluten free? You're sure? You looked? And they're brown rice? Handmade? Libby, did you look?"

There isn't a dollar figure high enough to get me to take Libby's job.

"All right, Libby. If you're sure you've got the right thing. Are you sure, Libby? Okay. Come back to the office, Libby."

Katrina ended the call, releasing all of us from the weird tractor beam holding us in place. Fearing Katrina would make another call, I darted past the reception desk and down the hall to Peri's office.

She sat behind her desk looking chic and pulled together. I, on the other hand, must have looked a little shell-shocked because she said, "Katrina?"

"Yeah," I said, and dropped into the chair in front of her desk. "How can Libby stand to work for her?"

"Their relationship is bizarre," Peri said. "Libby used to model for KGE."

Libby had the figure and face for modeling so it surprised me that she'd stepped down to a personal assistant job when modeling paid so much better.

Sensing major gossip was in play, I asked, "Why the change?

What happened?"

Peri shrugged. "I don't know, exactly. I stay out of Katrina's business, and I don't know Libby well enough to ask."

Okay, that was disappointing. Still, I wasn't giving up so easily.

"Maybe I should mention a job change to Libby," I said.

"Don't waste your breath," Peri told me. She gestured to the L.A. Affairs portfolio I'd brought with me. "Is that the menu for the dessert stations?"

Huh. Somebody who worked in an office but didn't want to engage in office gossip? Weird.

I presented her with the menu and she looked it over. The caterer, one of my regulars, had done a bang-up job of putting together a wide selection of cookies, pastries, and cupcakes.

"Maybe some fruit?" Peri suggested.

Fruit? At a dessert station? Had I somehow phased into an alternate, less-chocolate-is-more universe?

Then I realized Peri was right. There was nothing like the presence of designer fashions and does-she-look-better-than-me concerns to make a woman up her fashion game, resurrect her New Year's resolution, and want to eat better and lose weight.

"Yes, I already made a note about adding fruit," I said.

It was a total lie, but so what?

Then, just to give my event planner extraordinaire reputation a bump, I added, "And some sugar-free items, of course."

I almost gagged when I said that.

"Great idea," Peri said and passed the menu back to me.

"So," I said, tucking it away and trying to sound casual. "How's everybody doing here? You know, after what happened yesterday?"

"That was really awful, wasn't it, Rayna falling like that," Peri said.

I took that to mean word hadn't spread through KGE that Rayna had been murdered—not yet, anyway.

"I didn't know Rayna very well," Peri said. "I handle the business end of things and do the client billing, along with anything else that gets dumped on my desk. I don't have much contact with the models unless there's a problem collecting their fee."

The inner workings of KGE were a mystery to me, but I

figured it was like most every other type of agency and they got a cut of whatever money their employees brought in.

"Had Rayna worked here long?" I asked.

"About a year or so, I think," Peri said. "She was one of our fit models."

When most people heard the term "fit model" they assumed it had something to do with working out, the gym, or some kind of exercise, which would seem odd given that Rayna was a plus-size girl.

Actually, a fit model was used by fashion designers and clothing manufacturers to check the fit of their designs on a real person, sort of like a living mannequin. They required very specific body types and measurements.

But the models didn't just wear the garments so the designer could check the fit. They gave input on the feel of the garment's fabric, how it moved, whether or not it was comfortable, all of which could make or break a fashion line.

It was a cool job to have—plus it paid a fortune, over a hundred bucks an hour. It had to, given that the models had to always maintain exacting measurements and stand for hours in different heel-heights while they were chalked, pinned, and talked about by a design team as if they were, in fact, a mannequin. A designer's entire fashion line was based on that model's specs. If she gained or lost even a fraction of an inch, it could completely throw off the fit of the garments, wreak havoc at the factory, and add additional costs.

"So you're short a model now," I said.

"We're short a number of people." Peri gestured to a stack of file folders on the corner of her desk. "IT techs, an admin assistant. We lost one of our two agents, so now Chrissie is handling the bookings for all of our models. And, of course, we need models."

"Katrina must be scrambling to hire replacements," I said.

Peri gave me a sour smile. "You'd think."

"I'm guessing the models are the hardest to find," I said.

"Plus-size girls are almost impossible to find. There are only a few working in all of L.A. Most are represented by an agency. A few are independent," Peri said.

I could see where going the independent route could be desirable, since the model could set her own fee and not worry about an agency's commission taking a bite out of her income.

"Actually, we're down two plus-size models now," Peri said. "Colleen was our go-to girl. She had a dozen clients and usually worked forty hours per week."

Wow, KGE must have been making major bucks off of Colleen.

"A model doesn't work for one specific designer?" I asked.

"Most of the models work for lots of different designers. You know, an hour here, two hours there, always traveling from place to place for a fitting," Peri said. "I guess Colleen had enough of dealing with the traffic and rushing to keep her appointments so she took a full-time job fitting for a designer in El Segundo."

Peri didn't say so but I knew that meant KGE had lost the commission Colleen brought in—unless, of course, KGE had another plus-size model that the designers felt could replace Colleen.

"What happened to her clients?" I asked. "Did she just leave everybody hanging?"

"That's the other sad part about Rayna falling down the stairs," Peri said. "Colleen had almost all of the plus-size jobs locked up, so Rayna had been getting just a few hours of work every month. But with Colleen out of the way Rayna could have picked up some, or maybe all, of her clients."

Rayna would have jumped from a few hours a month to thirty or forty per week? At a hundred-plus per hour? Wow, that would have been a major, life changing, I'm-hitting-the-mall increase.

"So who'll get those designers now?" I asked.

"Probably Ivy. She's our other plus-size. Her measurements were close to Colleen's. Rayna had almost identical measurements but with her gone, the designers will have to do minimal adjustments to their patterns and make-do with Ivy," Peri said. "At least the work won't be going to a different agency."

I knew what she really meant was that the model's commission wouldn't be going to another agency. Not that I blamed her, of course. Businesses, especially small ones, needed every dime they could get to stay afloat. KGE didn't have that problem, but there was no reason to let income slip away.

"Ivy must feel kind of bad that she's getting all the work just because Rayna died," I said.

"I doubt it," Peri told me. "All the fit models usually get along---not her and Rayna. Ivy is very competitive. They were always competing for whatever bookings Colleen couldn't handle."

My senses jumped to high alert.

"Ivy will have it made now, with Rayna out of the picture," Peri said.

"Good for Ivy," I said.

But what I was really thinking was, good for me. I'd found my first murder suspect.

Chapter 5

I left the KGE office—thankfully, Katrina was nowhere in sight—and headed for the staircase at the front of the building. Halfway there, I stopped.

The security guard was probably in the lobby—hopefully he was providing some actual security now, considering somebody had gotten murdered on his watch—and I wasn't all that anxious to subject myself to his I-know-you-did-it stare. I decided this was a good time to check out the info I'd just received from Peri about Ivy and Rayna competing for the clients who'd just become available, thanks to Colleen's departure from KGE.

Money, of course, was one of the top motives for murder. Major bucks were in play. I didn't like thinking Ivy had resorted to killing someone, but greed did crazy things to people.

I pulled out my cell phone and checked the KGE website. I wanted to get a look at Ivy, my new murder suspect, so I clicked on the fit models tab. The images of three girls, all dressed in black leggings and tank tops, appeared along with their first names and statistics.

One of them was Rayna. It made me kind of sad seeing her like this, smiling, posing, showing off her figure, a look of happiness on her face hinting that she knew better things were coming her way. Now she was dead—and not just dead, murdered.

It irked me that KGE's IT team didn't have their stuff together enough to have already taken down her photo. Then I saw that Colleen's picture was still on their site, too. What were those guys doing, playing *Call of Duty* all day? Yeah, okay, Peri had told me the agency was short on IT techs, but still.

Maybe Katrina should pay more attention to this kind of thing, and less to the hunt for handmade, gluten-free, brown rice tortillas.

Libby would likely appreciate the break.

The other model pictured on the site was Ivy. She looked to be around my age, maybe a couple of years older, and had long blonde hair.

Then it hit me—I'd seen her before. On the day of Rayna's murder, I'd seen Ivy seated in the KGE lobby when I'd arrived for my meeting with Peri.

Then something else hit me—she wasn't there when I left.

Oh my God. Was I looking at a murderer?

In my head, a vision appeared of Rayna running into Ivy at the top of the staircase, an argument breaking out over which of them would take over Colleen's clients, an argument that escalated into a physical altercation that sent Rayna tumbling to her death.

Maybe it had been an accident. Maybe it hadn't. But I could see it happening.

All I needed was some evidence.

I still wasn't up for dealing with the security guard down on the first floor, so I headed for the steps at the rear of the building. As I passed the staircase where Rayna had died—which kind of creeped me out—Libby came rushing up the steps.

She had on a black and white checked skirt and a white sweater that—yikes!—I'd seen at Holt's, and she carried a department-store-brand shoulder bag and a backpack with the KGE logo on the front. A few strands of hair had come loose from her bun. She seemed slightly out of breath as she rushed past me.

"Libby?" I called.

She whipped around and spotted me.

"Oh, yeah, Haley. Hi," she said, and started walking away.

Libby always seemed slightly frazzled—I suppose anyone would who had to deal with Katrina all the time.

"Are you okay?" I asked.

Libby didn't look any worse now than at the other times I'd seen her. But I hoped she could give me some intel on what was going on with Rayna and Ivy, and feigning concern—yes, I know, it wasn't very nice of me but oh well—seemed like a good way to get the spill-your-guts ball rolling.

Libby turned back. "Yeah, sure, I'm fine."

"I thought maybe you were upset about being here," I said, gesturing to the staircase. "You know, after what happened to Rayna yesterday."

"Oh."

Libby eyed the stairs, then looked at me and straightened her shoulders, pulling herself together, it seemed.

"We always use this staircase," she said. "The employee parking is downstairs, just outside the door."

I hadn't realized that. It meant that, if what I suspected was true, Ivy could have slipped in and out of the building without the security guard at the front desk knowing she was on the premises.

Libby walked a little closer. "Yes. Yes, of course what happened is upsetting. I'm very upset. It's terrible. Terrible."

"Did you know Rayna well?" I asked.

"I know all the models … kind of," Libby said. "They come into the office to drop off their vouchers."

"Vouchers?"

"You know, the paperwork the designers sign when they finish a fitting that tells how many hours they worked," Libby said. "Katrina has to review them before they go to Peri for billing. The models come in to pick up their paychecks, too, to save the mailing time."

"I guess everybody at the agency is pretty shaken up by what happened to Rayna," I said.

"I guess." Libby glanced down the hall. "I've got to go."

She was definitely not working with me, which was kind of annoying, so I tried another tactic.

"Listen, I know everybody here is busy, but Rayna's photo is still on the agency's website," I said. "You might want to make sure it's taken down."

Libby gasped and twisted her fingers together. "Oh my God, Katrina doesn't know, does she?"

"I didn't tell her," I said.

"Oh. Okay. Well, thanks."

I waited, expecting Libby to bring forth some juicy piece of office gossip in exchange for the helpful little tidbit of info I'd just given her—something that I could twist into evidence in my murder investigation, of course—but she didn't say anything.

I hate it when that happens.

Either Libby really didn't have any useful information about the rivalry that existed between Rayna and Ivy, or she just wasn't picking up on my oh-so-subtle hints. I decided to move on.

"See you later," I said, and headed down the hallway.

"Haley?"

I turned back. Libby hesitated a few seconds, then walked over.

"There's a rumor going around," she said.

Okay, now we were rolling.

"Somebody said that maybe Rayna's fall wasn't an accident," Libby said.

Oh, crap. Not exactly what I needed.

"Where did you hear that?" I asked.

"Some of the girls were talking about it in the office," Libby said. She paused, glanced around, then leaned in and said, "I think maybe something was going on with Rayna."

My major-gossip-maybe-a-major-clue invisible antenna sprang up.

"Rayna had gotten mixed up in a problem ... a big problem ... with one of her clients," Libby said.

My brain jumped from investigative-mode to intrigued-mode.

"What kind of problem?" I asked.

Libby's finger twisting increased. "The fit models are with the designers for hours at a time, usually several days a week. They see and hear what's going on there. You know, the internal problems, the personnel issues."

Libby paused.

I hate it when somebody pauses right when they get to the good part.

"Yes?" I asked.

"Well, Rayna witnessed some kind of abuse going on. There was a big investigation, a really big investigation, and ... and now there's a lawsuit. She was supposed to testify."

"Which designer?" I asked.

Libby shook her head. "I don't know. Rayna didn't say."

"You heard this from Rayna? Directly?"

"Oh, yes. I saw her in the breakroom one day. She was upset, so she told me," Libby said. "Do you ... do you think it might have something to do with Rayna maybe getting killed?"

It was, of course, the first thing that had popped into my head.

"You told the homicide detectives, didn't you?" I asked.

"The detectives?" Libby's eyes widened. She shook her head frantically. "I can't let KGE get into trouble. I can't cause

Katrina a problem. She's a great person. She's wonderful. She gave me this job when I couldn't model anymore. Oh my God. *Oh my God.* If she hadn't done that—"

Libby was on the verge of going completely bat-crazy.

I'm not good with people who go completely bat-crazy.

"It's okay." I attempted to calm her down by waving my hands—which, by the way, almost never works—and said, "You're not going to get the agency in trouble. If there's a lawsuit, Katrina already knows about it. The detectives will find out. They're really good at doing background stuff."

Libby froze and clamped her mouth closed for a moment, then said, "I hadn't thought about that."

I was sure the homicide detectives would learn about the lawsuit in no time and, like me, they'd easily imagine some crazed fashion designer desperate to avoid a scandal and possible financial ruin getting rid of a witness who could bring years of work crashing down. Millions of dollars were at stake, as were the reputations and livelihoods of hundreds of people.

Libby's bat-crazy frenzy lessened slightly to semi-panic mode.

"You won't tell anybody, will you?" she asked. "Please, don't say anything. Katrina wouldn't want word getting out. You know how people talk, how they stretch things, make them into something they're not."

Of course I knew, given that I was occasionally one of those people—not something I was particularly proud of, but there it was.

Libby came closer, looking more desperate, and reached for me. For an instant I thought she might grab me, drop to her knees, and beg.

"It's okay," I said, backing up a few steps. "I won't say anything."

"I just ... I can't let Katrina down," Libby said.

Libby had mentioned that Katrina had given her a job when she couldn't model anymore. I'm sure that meant a lot to Libby—as it would to anyone—but to have instilled this kind of loyalty in her seemed over the top.

But maybe not, I realized. People did all kinds of crazy things when they needed a job, when they were facing a financial crisis and staring head-on into their lives changing for the worse.

Who was I to question Libby's actions? After all, I'd taken a job at the crappier-than-crappy Holt's Department Store when I'd needed money.

"Don't worry," I said, then forced a little smile. "I don't work here, remember? Who would I tell?"

Libby seemed to relax a little and offered a faint smile in return.

"You're right," she said, then glanced down the hallway and seemed to spin herself up again. "I've got to go."

She didn't say good-bye or wait for a response from me, just yanked her KGE backpack higher on her shoulder and hurried away.

I couldn't bring myself to use the staircase Rayna had died on, so I walked to the rear of the building and took the stairs to the first floor. The smell of paint hit me immediately.

Clark flashed in my head. He'd been rambling around in my thoughts since yesterday. I wondered if he'd heard anything more about Rayna's death. I decided I should talk to him again—strictly in the line of duty, of course, not because he was really good looking.

None of the offices at this end of the building were occupied—not surprising since the views here were of other buildings, making them less desirable to tenants. I glanced down the long hallway to the lobby and the front entrance. Several people were coming and going. The security guard stood at his post, his back to me.

The smell of fresh paint led me to the space across the hall from the staircase. The door was open. Inside was a suite of offices, one large, main room with a corridor leading to what I guessed were smaller offices, and maybe a breakroom and restrooms.

The main room held no furniture. Drop cloths, paint buckets, and all kinds of equipment were stacked in the corner. The walls were I-have-no-imagination-white.

There was no sign of Clark but I figured that since the door was open, he had to be here somewhere.

"Hello?" I called, as I crossed the room.

I headed down the narrow corridor past two small offices. The doors stood open and I saw that the walls were painted a trendy pale gray. I walked farther down the hall to an office at the rear of the suite. A ladder was set up and painting equipment was positioned around the room. One of the walls was covered in gray. Still, no sign of Clark.

I was no professional painter but I could see that he was changing the color of the office walls from white to gray, and that he'd started with the offices at the rear of the suite and was working his way toward the main room.

A thought zinged into my head.

Yesterday, had Clark really left his work—possibly climbed down a ladder and put aside his brush or roller—to walk into the corridor over and over to look down the hall? For what—or, more likely, who? Who could he have been expecting to see approaching?

Who could have been *that* important?

This end of the building was quiet. None of the offices were occupied. Had anybody actually seen what Clark had been doing?

Another, slightly disturbing thought flew into my head.

Was it just an incredible coincidence that Clark had looked down the hallway and seen Rayna lying at the foot of the staircase at the same moment I rushed down to check on her?

I hadn't seen him come out of the office. He'd just suddenly appeared.

An uneasy feeling shot through me. I turned to leave.

Clark blocked the doorway.

Chapter 6

Yesterday, I'd thought how good looking Clark was. Tall, with broad shoulders and bulging biceps that resulted from hours of painting. He must have been incredibly strong. Now, with him looming over me, blocking the doorway, I thought how he easily he could have hurled Rayna down the staircase.

"Hungry?" he asked, and held up the pizza box he'd brought in with him. "Pepperoni. It's a classic."

Clark smiled easily and fished a can of soda from his pocket. "There's a vending machine next door. I can get you something to drink, if you'd like."

Aside from his intimidating size and my completely unfounded suspicion, he came across like an okay guy. Still, I kept my invisible something's-not-right-here defensive shield up, thinking I might be able to get some info from him.

"No, thanks," I said. "But you go ahead and eat. Don't let it get cold."

He balanced the pizza box on top of a five-gallon paint can and popped the top on his soda.

"Good color," I said, gesturing to the walls.

Clark grinned. "Every color starts to look like every other color after I've spent hours staring at it."

"Do you work for the building management company?" I asked.

He shook his head. "I'm filling in. The guy who was supposed to handle the job had a family problem."

"And one of the days you're here, somebody gets killed," I said, trying for what-are-the-chances irony.

"Yeah, look, I still feel bad about the cops coming down on you," he said. "They haven't been back, have they?"

Was he genuinely concerned about me? Or was he fishing for some info about the investigation?

"I haven't heard from them," I said. "Have you?"

"Not a word," he said, and sipped his soda.

Either he didn't know anything more or he was really good at holding back—neither of which suited me.

"Have you talked to any of the models from KGE?" I asked.

"Not likely. I don't get a lot of women willing to talk to me when I smell and look like this," he said. "So either you're nose-blind, or a really nice person."

"I'm not nose-blind," I told him. "And I'm not all that nice."

He gave me a that's-cool nod. We looked at each other for a while and I got the feeling something was sparking between us, like maybe he was about to ask me to go out with him.

The thought startled me. Why would I think something like that? I hardly knew the guy and, earlier, I'd gotten a he-could-be-trouble vibe from him. Plus, I was kind of seeing Liam. We were dating and it wasn't serious—we hadn't discussed being exclusive, but still.

A cell phone dinged. I noticed then that it was sitting atop one of the unopened cans of paint.

"I see you found your phone," I said. He looked confused so I added, "Yesterday, in the hallway. You didn't have it."

"It always turns up," he said.

"By the way, did whoever you were waiting for yesterday show up?" I asked.

"You've got a great memory," Clark said. "Remind me never to try and pull anything over on you."

"You'd better remember that on your own," I told him.

He grinned, then said, "I've got to get back to work."

He backed out of the room, my invitation to leave, obviously. He followed me through the office suite to the main corridor and the door that led out the rear of the building.

"I guess I'll see you around," he said, as he held the door open and I walked outside.

"How much longer will you be working here?" I asked.

He shrugged. "A while."

I walked a few feet and glanced back. Clark stood in the doorway, watching. I waved; he waved, then disappeared inside.

Something didn't sit right with me about that guy—and I was sure it wasn't because of the paint fumes I'd inhaled.

Clark had evaded most of my questions and he'd given me no new info. Was he hiding something? Or was he a nice guy who simply didn't want to give up a lot of info to somebody he'd just met?

I couldn't be sure so I added Clark's name to my mental suspect list. Now, all I needed was some evidence.

I remembered that Libby had mentioned the employee parking lot was located near the side exit, so I circled the building. I spotted a van with the name "Paint Masters," along with contact info and a cool logo featuring cans of paint, on the side. I pulled out my cell phone and snapped a pic.

After the day I'd had so far, I decided I definitely deserved a Starbucks—really it takes very little for me to decide I deserve a Starbucks—so I headed for Lankershim Boulevard.

When I'd left L.A. Affairs earlier I'd had no suspects in Rayna's murder. Now I had several.

For starters, there was Ivy, Rayna's rival for all the clients who'd come available thanks to Colleen's departure from KGE. Ivy had an excellent motive for doing away with Rayna. Plus, Peri had told me that she and Rayna didn't get along.

One of the parties in the lawsuit that Rayna had gotten involved with might definitely benefit by eliminating her as a witness. I'd have to find out what that whole thing was about and put a name to a suspect.

I waited at the corner for the light to change, then crossed with the other pedestrians.

Thinking about the lawsuit made me think of Liam, which was definitely more pleasant than my mental list of murder suspects—except that I felt just the tiniest bit guilty about my sort-of-kind-of attraction to Clark even though, technically, it was in the line of duty.

I considered asking Liam to dig up some info on the lawsuit that involved Rayna. He was an attorney and had ready access to that sort of info, but he was also a stickler about confidentiality—which was admirable but inconvenient for me.

By the time I reached Starbucks I'd nixed the notion of asking Liam for help. I'd get the info from another source, somehow.

I ordered my drink, paid with my awesome gold card, and headed outside again. The afternoon was beautiful so I decided that everything at L.A. Affairs could wait a bit longer while I indulged in two of my favorite things—a mocha frappuccino and shopping.

I window-shopped my way along Magnolia Boulevard, checking out the fashions. Just as I stopped to admire a terrific display of maxi skirts—wham—it hit me that Libby might have a motive for murdering Rayna.

That kind of thing just happens to me.

It's a gift, really.

Libby was totally devoted to Katrina—which I still didn't get, despite the whole she-gave-her-a-job-thing—so I could see how Libby would want to shield Katrina from any sort of trouble. Having one of the KGE models involved in a lawsuit with a design company could have a major impact on the agency. Designers would be reluctant to book KGE models. Girls would think twice about signing with the agency, fearful it might somehow lead to legal entanglements.

Had Libby, due to some screwball sense of loyalty, killed Rayna to end KGE's involvement in the lawsuit?

I headed down the street and drained the last of my brain-boosting chocolate, sugar, and caffeine frappie, hoping it would be enough to keep me going, and tossed the cup in a trashcan.

I thought back to the day of the murder. When I'd left my meeting in Peri's office and returned to the lobby, Ivy was missing and Libby had rushed in looking panicked and scattered. Was that because she'd just pushed Rayna down the stairs?

Honestly, Libby most always looked panicked and scattered. And being thankful for a job and loyal to your boss was a long way from murder.

Still, I added her to my you-might-have-done-it-but-I-have-no-evidence heap of suspects.

I crossed the street and walked along Lankershim again. Something about the day Rayna was killed kept hopping around in my head but I hadn't been able to pin it down. Then my thoughts shot off in an unexpected direction.

Peri had arrived late for our meeting despite always being punctual. It was totally unlike her. Could she have murdered Rayna?

Yeah, I suppose she could have, but why?

I had no idea. Jeez, this whole murder investigation was—

Wait. Hang on.

I froze on the sidewalk. My gaze locked onto a shop window.

Handbags. Gorgeous handbags. Gorgeous beyond all reason handbags. Oh my God, how had I not noticed this store before?

I dashed to the display window. Inside were three bags, each distinctively styled and heavily embellished with exquisite details. These were unique, one-of-a-kind handbags made of tapestry, silk, velvet, wool, and other I-can-die-happy-now fabrics. They were chic, classic, trendy, and edgy—and soon they would be mine.

Immediately, I knew exactly what kind of outfit I should wear with each of the bags. The visions exploded in my mind.

Then something else hit me.

I could take one of the clutches to my cousin's wedding and finally--*finally*—give everyone in my family something fabulous to say about me.

Oh my God, I absolutely had to call Marcie and share this must-see-and-drool moment.

I raced to the door and pushed. It didn't budge.

What the heck?

Oh my God, the place was closed? In the middle of the afternoon? How could this happen?

I stepped back and saw a small sign discretely placed on the door that read designs by darby, appointments available.

I felt slightly light-headed.

Oh, wow. This wasn't merely a shop offering artisan bags— it was an exclusive handbag shop, catering to an upscale, discerning clientele. The fashion-elite shopped here—and I totally deserved, and absolutely *had*, to get inside.

I paced along the storefront peering through the windows at the shelves and display tables inside. Through a door on the rear wall I spotted a workroom, the place where handbag-magic happened. The space was cluttered with bolts of fabric, embellishments, a sewing machine, and several handbags in various stages of completion.

The urge to get inside, see everything up close, feel the fabrics, touch the ribbons, bows, and buttons, nearly overwhelmed me.

I whipped out my cell phone and called the number on the sign. A recording picked up and a woman identifying herself as Darby invited me to leave a message. I stated that I was interested in her designs and managed to sound discerning and

—

upscale—which meant I didn't scream.

I hung up, took a photo of the bags in the display window, and sent it to Marcie. I knew she would flip-out—as a BFF and fellow handbag aficionado would—when she saw them.

A few minutes passed while I tried to calm myself—I'm not really good at calming myself—drawing in some deep breaths and trying to relax. Darby might call me back at any moment and I feared she might refuse to grant me an appointment if I sounded like a crazed psycho.

Not that I blamed her, of course.

Deep breaths and relaxation attempts did nothing to calm me, so I decided it was best to move along with my day. I needed to get back to my office at L.A. Affairs. I had a number of events to handle and tending to them would keep my mind off of the gorgeous handbags. Probably. Maybe. Well, it was worth a try.

I headed down the sidewalk, then froze.

Walking toward me was the second most gorgeous thing I'd seen today—Jack Bishop.

Chapter 7

Jack Bishop was a private detective, a guy so hot he deserved his own TV series. He was tall, built, and had gorgeous eyes and dark hair. Today he had on nice pants, a collar-shirt, and a sport coat.

I'd met Jack at one of my many I-thought-that-would-have-turned-out-better jobs, a law firm where I worked in accounts payable and he'd done consulting work. We'd joined forces on several cases—what I liked to think of as a superhero team. There had always been some sort of spark between us but we'd kept it professional because I'd been involved with my now-ex-official-boyfriend Ty; I'm a complete old lady about that sort of thing.

"I was at the agency," Jack said, nodding in the direction of KGB's office.

Jack's firm was handling security for the fashion crawl, so I figured he'd been there to discuss something with Peri.

"I must have just missed you," I said.

"I knew I'd find you here," Jack said, nodding toward the handbags in the shop window.

True, my obsession with handbags was legendary.

"Awesome detecting skills," I told him. "But you could have just called me."

Jack edged closer. "I like the hunt."

Oh my God, he used his Barry White voice. I'm totally helpless against his Barry White voice.

Still, I resisted the urge to melt down into a puddle right there on the sidewalk and said, "Any problems with security?"

I'd recommended Jack and his team to provide security for the crawl—and not just because he was so good looking. Really. Well, okay, kind of.

"Other than the murder?" he asked.

I'd seen nothing on the news about Rayna's death, and Peri thought it had been an accident, but somehow Jack knew about it and also knew the homicide detectives were calling it a murder.

—

Jack was like a security ninja, somehow learning everything that went on.

"I found the body," I said.

He gave me a don't-bother-because-I-already-know-everything-you're-involved-with look which, while probably true, didn't suit me—or else it was flattering. I wasn't sure which.

"I don't think it's connected to the crawl," I told him. "There were some internal problems at the model agency."

I gave him the rundown on the rivalry between Rayna and Ivy over the new clients that had come available. He listened and I could almost see his brain working, which was totally hot, of course.

"What else?" he asked.

No way was I going to mention my suspicion about Clark, Libby, or Peri since I'd discovered no evidence that any of them had committed the crime, and I didn't want to look like a total idiot in front of Jack.

"Rayna was involved in a lawsuit," I said.

Yeah, okay, I'd promised Libby I wouldn't tell anyone about the info she'd shared with me. But I wasn't spouting idle gossip to a co-worker in the breakroom—which, honestly, I'd done a zillion times—and this was possibly a crucial lead in a murder investigation.

"Who told you?" Jack asked, after I explained what I'd learned.

At this point there was no reason to hold back so I said, "Libby. She's Katrina's personal assistant."

He nodded, taking in the info, seeming to mentally file it away with everything else I'd told him.

"Have you heard anything?" I asked.

Jack wasn't one to share a lot of info, which irked me at times, but after the leads I'd discovered and reported, he had no reason not to give up what he knew.

"The detectives don't have much," he told me. "No problems in her personal life, no boyfriend stalking her, no unhappy roommate, no psycho ex-husband. No drug or alcohol abuse. She waitressed and tended bar at a couple of restaurants. Came to work on time. Did her job. Didn't cause trouble. She was generally well liked. Not a single red flag."

I wasn't sure how Jack had gotten the inside scoop on the

official investigation. It was just more of his security wizardry which was way cool since I benefited from it.

Still, it made me sad thinking about Rayna, a single girl working hard to make a life for herself who had met such a tragic end. It made me even more sad thinking that she'd been about to get the break of a lifetime with all the new clients who'd come available, and the big bucks she would have made.

I didn't want to think about that anymore, so I said, "What's going on with the crawl? Any problems?"

"Situations," Jack said, nodding toward the street. "Homeless are living in some of the buildings."

As with any densely packed city, a number of buildings were unoccupied. Several of them had been rented for the crawl and their ground floors would be used for the pop-up showrooms and other events.

"Most of these places have been sitting empty for months," Jack said. "The owners haven't done much to keep people out."

"That's one of the reasons they were so anxious to jump onboard the crawl," I told him. "Some of the owners want to unload the buildings. They're hoping the attention will draw buyers or at least some tenants."

Jack glanced down the street at the four- and five-story buildings, and I figured we were thinking the same thing: no way would anybody want to be stuck with an unoccupied space that cost a fortune every month to maintain.

"Everything will be handled in time for the crawl," Jack told me. "Don't worry."

"I'm not worried."

I never worried about anything that involved Jack. He was that kind of guy.

We stood there staring at each other, some weird kind of spark passing between us, the same spark that neither of us had ever acted on.

Jack's cell phone chimed. He pulled it from the inside pocket of his sport coat, glanced at the screen, then put it away again. I figured he had a meeting or something, but didn't want to cut our conversation short. Nice.

Still, I didn't want to delay him, and I sure didn't want to hear him say that he had to go.

"I have to get back to work," I said.

He walked me to my Honda that I'd left in a parking lot down the street, opened the door, then closed it after I dropped into the driver's seat. I buzzed the window open. He braced his hands on the door and leaned down.

"I'll see what I can turn up on that lawsuit," he said.

"Great. You'll let me know?"

He hesitated a few seconds, then said, "I know this isn't going to do any good, but I have to say it—don't get involved with this murder investigation. It's dangerous."

"I know. You're right."

Jack's eyebrows crept up. "I'm right? You're not going to get involved?"

"You're right that it's dangerous."

He huffed. "But you're not backing off."

"The police aren't making any progress. I can't run the risk that the investigation might go sideways and I could be named a suspect. The crawl could be impacted or even cancelled." I managed a tiny smile. "They note things like that in our personnel file."

Jack's expression hardened and I knew what I'd said didn't suit him, which was slightly irritating but gave me a warm feeling at the same time.

"Then keep me informed about what's going on," Jack told me. "I don't care how stupid you think it sounds, I want to hear it."

This, of course, would have been the perfect time to tell him that I had several other names on my mental list of suspects, but doing so would announce that I'd withheld the info earlier. I always say that timing in life is important—and this didn't seem like the time to share my suspicions.

"I will," I told him.

Jack gave me a you'd-better glare, which was totally hot, of course.

I started the car and shifted into reverse. Jack stayed where he was, watching me. Finally, he stepped back.

I pulled out of the parking spot and glanced in my rearview mirror. Jack was still watching.

My cell phone buzzed as I headed down Magnolia toward the freeway. Mom was calling.

No way could I deal with her and listen to the latest gossip about my overachieving cousins, so I let the call go to voicemail. Yeah, okay, I know that wasn't very nice, considering that she was my mom, but there it was.

Right now my head was filled with images of Jack—honestly, how could it not be? Then, of course, my ex-official-boyfriend Ty popped in there, and I definitely didn't want to think about him. Clark appeared in my thoughts and I didn't feel so great thinking I was kind of attracted to a guy who might be a murderer—and that caused me to think about my sort-of boyfriend Liam and how maybe I was technically, though not officially, mentally cheating on him by thinking about Clark.

Good grief.

My life needed an ejection seat.

I hit the onramp to the 170, determined to focus on the work that lay ahead of me at L.A. Affairs. Honestly, I liked my job and I was pretty darn good at it. At the moment, organizing events for total strangers so they could have a fabulous occasion with friends and family that would not include me seemed preferable to thoughts of all those men, plus my mom—and a murder—that were swirling in my brain.

But as I was mentally reviewing the things I'd have to take care of when I arrived at my office, the image of yet another man materialized in my head—and this one might actually do something that would help.

I grabbed my cell phone and called Detective Shuman.

* * *

"Have you been studying?" Sandy asked.

I looked at her as if she'd lost her mind—because I actually thought she'd lost her mind.

I was folding towels in Holt's housewares department letting the image of the awesome handbags I'd spotted yesterday in the display window in North Hollywood fill my head, when Sandy walked up and startled me back into the somewhat depressing present moment.

"You know, studying," she said, looking incomprehensibly excited, considering where we were.

Bad enough that I'd spent my Saturday afternoon and evening here, so no way was I going to put mental effort into anything beyond my internal count-down to the store closing.

Sandy seemed to pick up on my I'm-totally-lost expression, as a BFF would, and said, "You know, for the contest. Remember? They told us about it in the meeting."

I've really got to get better about paying attention in meetings.

Or not.

Then it hit me—she was talking about the Holt's contest and the looming threat of winning a crappy beach towel, not to mention the unveiling of the store's new fashion line.

I had no clue what any of that had to do with studying.

"Everybody's really into it," Sandy said, waving her hands around the store. "I figured you'd be going for it, too."

Like she just met me, or something.

I must have looked even more lost now—which I totally was—because Sandy said, "You can do it, Haley. You know all about customer service. You worked in the booth with Grace and—"

A jolt like a zap of electricity hit me as I realized the true meaning of this can-my-day-get-any-worse moment.

"The contest is about customer service?" I asked.

I might have said that kind of loud.

Sandy drew back a little.

Yeah, I'd screamed it.

"Sorry," I said.

She rolled with it and said, "That's why everybody is studying. We have to answer questions about the store. You know, where the merchandise is located, the brands we carry, our return policy, the best way to help a customer. That kind of thing. Then we take a test on a computer that—"

I stopped listening.

My own personal customer service policy was in direct opposition to Holt's official position, so no way could I even come close to winning anything in the contest—and that suited me just fine.

Sandy gave me a let's-don't-get-in-trouble look and gasped softly. "Look out. Here comes Rita."

Sandy took off. I started folding towels again, managing an I'm-busy-but-I'm-not-knocking-myself-out pace.

Rita glared at me as she walked past. Since I was in no mood to deal with her, I channeled my beauty pageant mom's I'm-better-than-you air and ignored her.

As Rita disappeared into the kids' clothing department, I felt my cell phone vibrate in the back pocket of my jeans. We're not supposed to have our phones on the sales floor, but oh well.

My first thought was that it might be Mom calling to update me on my cousins and the latest wedding gossip. I was still avoiding her for obvious reasons. Of course, I didn't want to miss an important call—like Marcie wanting to go shopping, or something—so I dashed down the aisle, pushed through the double doors into the stockroom, and yanked my phone out of my pocket in one smooth, well-practiced motion.

The ID screen showed that Darby was calling.

I nearly dropped my phone.

Oh my God. Darby of Designs by Darby. Those awesome, fabulous, I-could-actually-die-if-I-don't-get-one handbags I'd seen in the NoHo shop window.

I hit the green button.

"Hello." I might have said that a little too loud.

"Uh, hello?" a meek voice replied.

Okay, I'd actually screamed my greeting.

I drew in a deep breath trying to calm myself—where was Marcie at a time like this?—and let it out slowly.

"Yes, hello," I said, managing to find my I'm-not-really-a-psycho voice. I introduced myself and said, "I saw your handbags in your shop window. I'm very interested in them."

"Thank you," she said.

"Could I make an appointment to visit your shop?"

Silence on the line. Oh my God, was she wondering if I really was a psycho? Was she thinking she'd need back-up for our appointment? Had I blown my chance to get my hands on one of her gorgeous bags?

Another few seconds dragged by, then Darby said, "How about tomorrow at two?"

I almost collapsed.

"Perfect," I said. "I'll see you then."

We ended the call and I did a combination of double fist pumps and the Snoopy happy dance worthy of *Dancing WithThe Stars*.

Oh my God, I had to call Marcie. She'd definitely have to go with me. Tomorrow couldn't get here soon enough. I could lose myself in all those gorgeous handbags and select the perfect one to take to my cousin's wedding. Maybe I'd buy two bags—no, wait, three, maybe more.

This was so totally awesome. I didn't know how my day could get any better.

Then it did.

Sandy pushed open the stockroom door and said, "There's a really hot guy outside looking for you.

Chapter 8

My first thought was to wonder who the hot guy waiting outside the stockroom might be. No way did I question Sandy's call, though. She knew a hot guy when she saw one.

The image of Ty, my ex-official boyfriend bloomed in my mind. I ignored it.

Sandy pushed through the door and disappeared into the store, and Detective Shuman walked into the stockroom.

There was a guy-next-door ease about Shuman. He was taller than me, barely over the hump into his thirties, with dark hair and casual good looks. Some sort of low current always ran between us, one we'd never acted on because ... well, because of a number of things. We'd had our difficult moments—he was, after all, a homicide detective—but we'd managed to arrive at some sort of understanding.

I'd called Shuman and asked if he could nose around a bit, maybe get some inside info on Rayna's murder investigation from the detectives who were working the case, but I hadn't heard back from him. I wasn't expecting to see him tonight, but like I always say, you never know when something good is going to happen to you.

I noticed then that he wasn't dressed in his usual slightly mismatched shirt-tie-sport-coat combo but instead had on black jeans and a gray Henley shirt. Definitely a date-night look.

A thread of envy zipped through me. Saturday night. I was stuck working at Holt's. Why wasn't I going out?

"Hi, Haley," he said, and walked over.

"Still seeing Brittany?" I asked.

Shuman grinned—I love his grin—and said, "I'm on my way to her place."

I'd met Brittany and I liked her, and I was happy for Shuman.

"So, Rayna Fuller," Shuman said.

He'd shifted into cop-mode. I'd rather have gotten some info about how things were going with him and Brittany, but I went with it.

"Anything turn up in the investigation?" I asked.

He shrugged. "Nothing. Absolutely nothing."

Jack had told me pretty much the same thing, which meant that finding Rayna's killer anytime soon didn't look promising.

"One possible lead," Shuman said. "Someone fled the scene."

Oh, crap. That was *me*.

Yeah, this investigation was definitely in trouble.

"What have you turned up?" he asked.

I was flattered that Shuman thought I'd come up with something when the homicide detectives assigned to the case hadn't.

"A couple of things," I said, and gave him the rundown on the rivalry between Rayna and Ivy for the new clients, and the lawsuit she'd been involved with.

Shuman did his usual cop-nod, taking it in, running it through his cop-brain, and said, "What else?"

He knew me well enough to realize I was holding back, which irked me a bit for some reason. I didn't like being so transparent—or maybe I was just annoyed that he looked handsome tonight, was going on a date, and I wasn't.

Yes, I can be kind of shallow sometimes. I'm not proud of it, but there it was.

"Just a weird feeling I get from a few people," I said, and filled him in on my totally unsubstantiated, out-in-left-field suspicion about Clark, Libby, and Peri.

Shuman didn't look impressed. I couldn't blame him.

"So the investigation has turned up nothing on Rayna?" I asked. "Nothing? Nothing at all?"

I didn't want to think ill of Rayna, since I didn't even know her, but I was having trouble wrapping my head around the notion that she could be *so* wonderful that not one person had anything negative to say about her.

"The detectives talked to everybody at KGE, everybody at her other jobs, her family and friends," Shuman said. "They all said she was a great person. Everybody loved her."

"Really?"

Shuman shrugged as if he couldn't quite believe it either and said, "Really."

We were both quiet for a minute. I was still trying to get a grasp on how anybody could be that nice all the time when Shuman took a step back toward the stockroom door.

"I'll see what else I can turn up," he promised.

We left the stockroom together and walked to the front of the store.

"Tell Brittany I said hi," I told him.

Shuman gave me one final grin, and headed out.

I stood there for a few minutes, staring outside. It was dark now. The security lighting in the parking lot wasn't anything to brag about, casting everything in deep shadows. Vehicles pulled in and out of spaces and drove through the aisles. The store would close in a few minutes but several customers straggled in. I watched Shuman until he disappeared among the parked cars.

Ty flew into my head again. No way could I think about that whole thing, so I pushed him out of my thoughts—not always an easy thing to do, especially tonight.

I forced the image of my kind-of boyfriend Liam into my brain. We hadn't seen much of each other lately because he was preparing for a big case. At least, that's what he told me. He'd apologized and promised to make it up to me.

I chose to think it was true—not that he'd lost interest in our turtles-move-faster relationship—and that he wasn't on a date tonight with someone else. I'd told him it was okay, that he should work on his case, and that I already had plans for a fun evening with friends, which wasn't true, of course. I just didn't want to look like I was waiting around for him to ask me out.

I milled around in the junior's clothing department pretending to size a rack of dresses until Rita's voice over the P.A. announced that the store was closing. Customers drifted out. The cashiers shut down their registers.

Liam flew into my head again. I pulled my cell phone out of my pocket and checked for messages. Maybe he'd sent me something really thoughtful and caring since it was Saturday night—everyone's official date night—and we couldn't be together. I looked at the screen. Nothing.

Okay, that was disappointing—which made me think of my relationship with Ty. No way did I want to dwell on that. Jack popped into my head, and I wondered what he was doing tonight. Was he on a date? Working a mega-cool case?

My spirits plummeted further—I mean, jeez, how could they

—

not? Even Shuman had a date tonight. He'd looked really handsome when he'd been at the store earlier talking about Rayna's death.

The memory of our conversation perked me up a little—which just shows how upset I was, if thoughts of a murder investigation could make me feel better—and I remembered how weird it had struck me that no one had said anything bad about Rayna. Nobody. Not one single person.

How could that be?

Then it hit me.

Maybe the cops weren't talking to the right people.

* * *

It was a Louis Vuitton day. Definitely a Louis Vuitton day.

Since it was Sunday and I wasn't working at Holt's, I'd selected a fashion-forward, trendy outfit of black cigarette pants, a white oversized shirt topped with a short gray jacket, and stiletto booties, all of which enhanced my look-at-me Louis Vuitton satchel.

Yes, I'd put a lot of effort into looking casual.

But what else could I do? I was on my way to meet Darby at her handbag boutique, so it was essential that I upped my fashion game to the max. What if she thought I wasn't worthy of her fantastic handbags? What if she refused to sell one to me?

No way could I deal with that—especially since Marcie wasn't with me. She'd had a family thing to do today—she had a great family and actually enjoyed spending time with them, which I simultaneously thought was weird and was a little envious of—so she couldn't join me.

It was majorly disappointing, plus a little troubling since Marcie's absence meant I'd have nobody there to hold me back and keep me from buying every handbag in the shop. I'd have to control myself.

I'm not good at controlling myself.

I parked my Honda in the lot near the KGE office and headed to the boutique. Clark flashed in my head as I passed the building and I wondered if he was inside, painting. I wondered, too, if Libby was on duty today and what outrageous errands Katrina might have her ping-ponging around town to accomplish.

My heartrate picked up as I approached the boutique and spotted the handbags in the window. My breath caught—yes, they were as fabulous as I remembered. I paused at the door, drew in a calming breath—which did absolutely no good—and was about to go inside when my cell phone buzzed.

I hate it when that happens.

I froze for a second, debating whether or not to answer, then grabbed it and checked the time. I was a few minutes early for the appointment, and since I didn't want to look anxious, I checked the caller ID screen. Mom was calling.

Crap.

No way did I want to talk to her right now.

I was about to ignore her call when it hit me that by now Mom's siblings had surely exhausted all of my cousins' fabulous, world changing, altruistic accomplishments. There couldn't be anymore great news to share—and make me feel like crap. I mean, really, how much more could they achieve?

Besides, I was about to purchase a chic, sophisticated handbag that would wow all my family members at the wedding. Nothing could ruin my day now. Not even talking to Mom.

"Good news about your brother," Mom announced when I answered.

I relaxed. Whew! If she'd called to share something about my brother, I would definitely want to hear it. He'd been stationed overseas for a long time, flying F-16s in the Middle East. I missed him.

"He's coming home for the wedding?" I asked.

"No," Mom said. "It's something even better."

From the I-can-brag-about-this-to-everyone tone in her voice, I doubted it would be something *better* for me.

"He's going to fly with the Thunderbirds," Mom said.

The Thunderbirds? My brother was going to be flying with the United States Air Force Thunderbirds? The aerial demonstration team that wowed spectators at air shows worldwide with their daring aerobatic maneuvers, whose pilots were the best of the best of the best?

Yeah, I was happy for my brother but—not to sound selfish—what about *me*? Now, not only would my mom have something to brag about at the wedding, my dad would, too.

Mom blabbed on but, honestly, I wasn't listening. I made

—

what might, or might not, have been appropriate remarks—I don't think Mom was listening, either—until we finally hung up. I dropped my cell phone into my handbag.

A minute or so passed, then I forced myself to rally.

I can do that when I have to.

Just steps away was a fantastic handbag boutique. Inside awaited an array of the most totally awesome bags ever conceived, and soon one—or more—of them would be mine. With it tucked into my hand, strategically positioned to call attention to it without looking showy, I would walk into that wedding and blow everyone away with my excellent taste.

I relaxed and opened the door. I could almost hear the handbags calling my name.

A wave of peacefulness washed over me as I stepped inside the boutique and took in the sights and scents of the luxury items. The shop was tiny yet elegantly appointed with about a dozen beautiful bags artfully displayed. In the corner was a seating group where clients could discuss and examine the purses in comfort. A cash register was discreetly situated on a small desk.

The brocade curtain over the doorway to the workroom parted and a young woman a few years older than me walked out. She was short, with red hair she'd twisted into a loose knot atop her head, and was dressed in chic Boho style in a denim jumpsuit over an orange T-shirt, four-inch platforms, and a print scarf that pulled the look together.

"You must be Darby," I said, and introduced myself.

"I'm really jazzed you like my work," she said.

We shared a we-love-handbags smile.

"I make all of them by hand in my workroom," Darby said, and nodded toward the room she'd just exited.

I glanced through the open curtain and saw bolts of fabric, an array of threads, and bins of what I guessed were embellishments and hardware for the purses. There was a big worktable, a sewing machine, and some other equipment I didn't recognize. Two partially completed handbags lay among the clutter.

Now that I was in Darby's boutique, this close to the fabulous bags, no way could I take a chance that she wouldn't think I was worthy of owning one. I had to impress her with my mad fashion skills.

"I'm one of the event planners for the fashion crawl," I said.

"Cool," she said and did, indeed, look impressed.

"I'm working with KGE Models," I said, and nodded in the direction of their office building.

Darby cringed slightly.

Yikes! Did that mean she knew Hurricane Katrina and now thought I was as crazy as she was? Did she deem me guilty by association and unworthy of one of her handbags?

I immediately shifted into back-down mode.

"Everybody who works there is really cool," I said. "Well, almost everybody."

Darby nodded. "I know a lot of the girls. They're in here all the time. The woman who runs the place is always a topic of conversation."

"Katrina."

"Hurricane Katrina," Darby said.

We shared a that-woman-is-crazy bonding moment, then Darby gestured to the handbags on display and asked, "Are you getting a gift for someone?"

"Yes," I said. "For myself."

She gave me a been-there smile. "A special occasion?"

"My cousin is getting married. It's a huge thing. Everybody in the family is attending," I said, then admitted, "I'm not looking forward to it."

As if she could read my mind, her face morphed into an I'm-so-sorry-you-have-to-go-through-that expression, and said, "Yeah, I know. My grandparents' fiftieth wedding anniversary is coming up. There's going to be huge party. Everybody will be there."

We shared a silent family-events-never-go-well moment.

"But you'll have one of your fantastic bags with you," I pointed out because, really, how could things go badly if you dressed and looked terrific?

"It would be better if I showed up with a date," Darby told me.

Her words hit home with me. I'd have to bring a plus-one to my cousin's wedding. At first blush, it would seem that asking my kind-of boyfriend Liam to attend with me would be the way to go. But I wasn't all that hot about subjecting him to my family, since I really liked him and didn't want to put him through their poorly disguised could-this-guy-finally-be-the-one

Q&A. And, of course, there was no way I wanted him to hear all the less than stellar remember-that-time things from my past that my family seemed hell-bent on always bringing up.

"Take your time looking at the bags," Darby said. "I'll be in the workroom if you have questions."

She disappeared through the curtained doorway, and I forced myself not to run to the displays. I channeled my mom's pageant walk, and glided across the shop.

Each handbag was unique. The fabric, hardware, and detailed styling—even the linings—were exquisite. The name of these heavenly creations was gracefully inscribed on a small placard alongside each bag.

Immediately, I loved every one of them. Oh my God, how would I ever choose? Jeez, I really needed Marcie here right now.

Then one of the bags practically jumped off of its display. It was a black beaded clutch with a white crystal clasp. Not only was it gorgeous, but it was the absolute perfect bag to compliment the dress I'd planned to wear to my cousin's wedding.

The little sign next to it indicated it was the Domino. I peeked inside and saw that it had a black and white polka-dot lining. It took everything I had not to scream. Oh my God, this was the one, the bag I absolutely had to have.

I must have made some sort of mewling sound—or maybe it was an actual scream—because Darby came out of the workroom.

"This one," I said, pointing and, I think, panting. "The Domino. This one. I *have* to have it."

Darby smiled, as another handbag lover would, and said, "It's one of my favorites."

The vision popped into my head of me gliding through my cousin's wedding, carrying the Domino, and everyone there seeing it and being totally jealous. Finally—*finally*—my family would have something great to say about me.

"I'll write up your order," Darby said and grabbed her iPad from the counter next to the cash register.

My excitement dipped. "I can't take this one?"

"It's for display. I make every bag individually for each client," she said, pecking on the keyboard.

"No, really, it's okay," I said. "I'm good with taking this one."

Darby shook her head. "I never let a display bag out of the shop. My clients get only top quality work, not a bag that's been sitting in a display window and has been handled by a lot of different people."

"Okay, that makes sense," I said, because, of course, I preferred a fresh bag. "I'll need it in two weeks."

Darby stopped typing.

I got a weird feeling.

She looked up at me. "The soonest I can get this bag for you is in six weeks."

"Six weeks?"

"I make each bag myself, no help from anyone. I have orders ahead of yours that I have to fill."

"Six weeks?"

"Sorry. That's the best I can do."

Oh, crap.

Chapter 9

Katrina appeared to be in major meltdown mode when I approached the KGE office on Monday morning and spotted her through the glass wall. She was in the lobby, waving her arms around and yelling at one of the models. My first thought was, of course, to run since it was way too early in the day to deal with one of her tirades.

But the model she was grilling looked young and scared. She was backed up against the wall, holding her backpack in front of her, looking like she either wanted to cry or suddenly develop a superpower that would allow her to disappear into a puff of smoke.

No way was I going to let that pass.

I burst through the office door and said, "Good morning, Katrina."

She either didn't hear me or didn't want to acknowledge my presence because she kept shouting.

"You're accountable," she told the model. "Each and every one of you is accountable and you're no exception."

Jeez, what was with the *accountable* thing? Katrina had been ranting about it—whatever it was—when I'd been here before.

"Katrina!" Yeah, I'd shouted her name.

She spun around, invisible how-dare-you daggers shooting from her eyes.

"Great news!" I gave her a huge I-don't-care-if-you-know-it's-fake smile. "Everybody loves your suggestions for the crawl! It's turning out fabulous!"

From her expression, I could see she had no idea who I was—not that I cared.

Behind her, the model saw her chance and broke for the door, just as I'd hoped she would.

"The fashion crawl is going to totally rock—all because of you!" I told her.

Now, not only did Katrina not know who I was, she also had no idea what I was talking about.

"Everybody is in awe of you," I said, then gave her a little finger wave. "Got to run."

While she was still standing there with her mouth slightly gaped open, I dashed down the hallway beside the receptionist's desk. I couldn't imagine that Katrina would follow me but if she did, I didn't want to drag Peri into the chaos by going into her office. Instead, I ducked into the breakroom.

The place looked like every other breakroom I'd been in—microwave, sink, cupboards, tables and chairs, a bulletin board with notices pinned to it. There was a refrigerator on the back wall. A girl was holding the door open, staring inside. She was tall, blonde, probably a few years older than me, dressed in black leggings and a black tank top. I recognized her from her photo on the KGE website. She was Ivy, one of the agency's plus-size fit models.

She was also one of my murder suspects—no, really, my prime suspect since she'd been competing with Rayna for the clients that had come available due to Colleen's departure from the agency. .

A this-is-perfect jolt zipped through me. Now was my chance to wheedle some information—and maybe a confession—out of her.

Just as I was ready to launch into my oh-so-clever questioning, Ivy slammed the refrigerator door and muttered, "Damnit."

She noticed me then but didn't seem surprised—or concerned. More like she could bite the head off of a small animal—or maybe me—at any moment.

"My snack is gone," she said and clenched her fists. *"Again!"*

"Somebody took your food?" I asked. Jeez, no wonder she looked so crabby. "Who'd do something like that?"

"Oh, I know who did it," Ivy said, her voice rising. "The same person who always takes it."

Okay, now I was outraged along with her.

"Who?" I demanded.

Ivy pressed her lips together, simmering, then said, "The office golden child, so there's nothing I can do about it."

"Who?" I asked again.

"Libby." Ivy shot the name at me as if firing it out of a

cannon. She huffed and puffed for another minute, then said, "I don't know if she's some kind of psycho, or just broke all the time."

Given what Libby continually put up with working for Katrina, I was leaning toward *psycho*. Yet I'd noticed that Libby's clothing and accessories were nowhere near as nice or fashion-forward as everyone else who worked at the agency, so maybe she had a problem managing her money.

"Libby should get a job that pays better," I said.

"She's so stupid. I can't stand her." Ivy opened one of the cupboards, then slammed the door. "Oh my God, I hate this place. There's never anything to eat in here anymore."

Before I could say anything—I was totally on board with needing plenty of snacks to get through the work day—Ivy spun around.

"Look at me. I'm plus-size. I can't lose weight. I get measured all the time. If I change, even a fraction of an inch, I don't fit my clients' specs and I'm out of a job. But Hurricane Katrina is too damn stingy to stock the snack cabinet anymore. She doesn't mind taking a huge chunk of my pay, though."

Ivy was waving her arms around and building to a full-blown snit fit, making this the perfect time to get information from her.

"And Katrina won't even make Libby stop stealing your food?" I asked.

That seemed to enrage Ivy further. She flung out both hands and said, "Katrina won't even process my pay vouchers on time. I have to come all the way here, hand in my vouchers instead of mailing them, so maybe—maybe—they'll get processed and I'll get paid in something close to a reasonable amount of time."

Peri had told me the models only got paid after their vouchers were processed, so I could understand why Ivy was ticked off about the delay. But before I could say anything, Ivy went on.

"I *knew* I should have gone with Chyna," Ivy said, clenching her fists.

"China?" I asked.

"I had my chance but no, I didn't take it. I thought I should be loyal, do the right thing. Emerald could have been *mine*."

Okay, I was totally lost. I had no idea what she was talking about. But she was on a roll. No way could I stop her.

"That's what I get for trying to be decent," Ivy grumbled.

"What does—"

Before I could ask anything, Ivy drew in another big breath and said, "Katrina will never get rid of Libby—never—no matter what she does. She's like Katrina's servant or slave, or something. Their relationship is totally whacked."

"Yeah, what's that all about?" I asked.

Ivy huffed. "Libby was in a car accident, I guess. I don't know, exactly. But she couldn't model anymore, so Katrina gave her a job as her personal assistant so she wouldn't have to move back home, and for that, Libby worships her."

"Would moving back home have been so bad?" I asked, thinking that nothing could be worse than working for Katrina.

"Some dinky little town in the Midwest?" Ivy made a gagging sound. "Libby was lucky to get away from that place. No way was she going back."

"I know Libby is loyal to Katrina, but it must creep her out a little to work here," I said, hoping I could bring the conversation around to my murder investigation. "Rayna died right here in the building. Everybody says she was such a nice person. And now she's dead. How awful is that?"

"Look," Ivy said, and yanked her backpack off the table. "All I know is that with Rayna gone, there're more clients for me."

"So the police must have questioned you," I said. "I mean, you had a motive and you were here that day."

I remembered that the day Rayna was killed, Ivy had been in the KGE lobby when I'd arrived for my meeting with Peri, but she was gone by the time our meeting ended—and that was just minutes before I found Rayna's body.

"Oh, like Rayna was murdered or something?" Ivy's sour expression turned into full-on bitch-face. "All those rumors are just a lot of crap. Everybody's got a theory about it, like maybe some crazed model-killer is on the loose, or she'd heard something she wasn't supposed to hear, or somebody was out to get her."

"You don't believe the rumors?"

"All I know is that Rayna fell down the stairs. Just her bad luck."

"Did you see her fall?" I asked.

—

"If I had, I would have called 9-1-1." Ivy slung her backpack over her shoulder and headed for the door, causing me to jump out of her way. She stopped, then spun back toward me. I braced myself.

She gasped and looked slightly embarrassed. "Oh my God, are you here for a job interview?"

Peri had told me the agency was short staffed. I hoped that whoever she hired would push for keeping snacks in the breakroom, for everybody's sake.

"No," I said, and told her my name. "I'm working with Peri on the fashion crawl."

"Well, that just figures. I knew Katrina wasn't trying to hire anyone," Ivy grumbled, her anger ramping up again. "Since Melody quit, the only agent we have now is Chrissie and she's not keeping up on everything. I missed out on two castings and she screwed up my bookings last week. I hate this place."

Ivy shoved past me and disappeared down the hallway.

Wow, she had some major anger issues going on.

Enough to have scuffled with Rayna, then pushed her down the stairs?

Definitely.

Plus, she hadn't mentioned having an alibi. She'd confirmed that Rayna was competition for the new clients that were in play, giving her a huge motive.

No way could I eliminate Ivy as a suspect in Rayna's murder.

But she had given me some new information. Rumors were making the rounds about Rayna, that someone was out to get her, or that she'd learned something she shouldn't know, putting her in danger.

Libby had confided in me that Rayna was being drawn into a lawsuit involving one of her clients. Could that be what those rumors were about? And if they were, who had started them?

I'd mentioned the lawsuit to Shuman, and Jack had told me he'd check into it. Why hadn't I heard back from them? I was, after all, *me*.

I grabbed my phone intending to call Jack when I spotted Peri walking past the breakroom doorway. She was probably looking for me, I realized, since I'd made an appointment with her before I'd left L.A. Affairs this morning.

"Sorry," I said, stepping into the hallway, "I was hiding out."

Peri nodded in the direction of the lobby. "Yes, I heard. Come on back."

I followed her to her office and we sat down. Her desk looked as neat and organized as always, though I did notice a few more stacks of folders. I hoped that meant she was interviewing perspective employees.

"I was talking to Ivy," I said. "She was pretty upset. Somebody stole her food out of the fridge. She seemed to think it was Libby."

"I'm not surprised," Peri said, tapping on her computer keyboard.

"Maybe Libby needs a pay raise," I said.

"She probably does," Peri agreed.

"I know you're shorthanded, but there must be somebody in H.R. who can make it happen."

"Libby doesn't work for the agency," Peri said. "She works for Katrina and is paid by her corporation."

"Oh."

I wasn't sure why that surprised me. I guess that since I'd only seen Katrina here at the agency, I hadn't thought about her having other business holdings.

Peri gestured to her computer screen and said, "Katrina made some additions to the menu."

I shifted into work-mode, and we discussed the changes Katrina wanted. It was nothing big but it made for one more thing that had to be handled before the menu could be finalized. Nothing an event planner extraordinaire like myself couldn't handle.

I totally rock at this job.

"I'll talk to the caterer and let you know if there's a problem," I said, as I rose from my chair.

"And I'll let you know if anything else changes," Peri said.

"Sounds good," I said, and left her office.

For a moment, I lingered in the hallway. I heard Peri on the phone talking in her usual slow, measured, nothing-can-shake-me voice. She was so calm, so unexcitable, so steady, I couldn't imagine her ever doing anything wild or crazy—or something as rash as arguing with Rayna, struggling with her enough to tear her shirt, then flinging her down the stairs. Maybe I'd been wrong suspecting Peri of her murder.

Yeah, sure, Peri had been unaccountably late for our meeting that morning and had the opportunity to murder Rayna, but since I hadn't discovered a motive, I wondered if I should mark her off of my she-might-have-done-it mental list of suspects.

The thought rambled around in my brain for a minute, then I decided that no, just because I hadn't uncovered a motive, didn't mean there wasn't one.

I headed down the hallway and slowed as I approached the lobby. I didn't hear any shouting so I knew Katrina wasn't there. As I left the KGE office and headed for the staircase at the front of the building, a thought that had been jarred loose by something Ivy had said in the breakroom planted itself front and center in my head. I stopped and pulled out my cell phone.

Detective Shuman and Jack had both told me that they'd found absolutely nobody in Rayna's past who didn't like her. In fact, everybody seemed to love her. No one thought ill of her. She was too good to be true.

Which, of course, meant that something was definitely wrong.

Nobody was that nice.

I'd thought before that they weren't talking to the right people, or asking the right questions. Somewhere, there was somebody willing and anxious to talk smack about Rayna. Ivy had unwittingly told me who that might be.

I accessed the KGE website on my cell phone, and saw that Rayna and Colleen's photos were still posted, which meant that IT was still down an employee and behind on everything. I opened the tab marked "agents" and saw pics of two women. One was Chrissie, the agent Ivy had mentioned this morning who was trying to handle the work of two people and was too overwhelmed to keep up on everything. The other was Melody Case, the agent who no longer worked for KGE.

Anybody who left a job, unless there was a confidentially agreement, was usually more than willing to dish dirt on their former employer. I figured Melody would be no exception—especially after working for Hurricane Katrina.

All I had to do was find her.

Chapter 10

As I left the KGB building I decided that since I was this close to Darby's handbag boutique, I'd stop by. Just to be friendly, of course—plus it wouldn't hurt for her to see my face again and maybe hurry along with making my handbag.

But first I had to contact Jack about locating Melody Case. I paused on the sidewalk, pulled out my cell phone and called. His voicemail picked up, which made me totally jealous because it probably meant he was doing something way cooler than I was. I left a message, trying for an I'm-cool-too vibe, asking him to call me back.

Just as I was about to drop my phone into my bag, it rang, which cheered me up thinking that if Jack had called back this quickly, maybe I really was the one having the coolest day, after all.

See how competitive I am?

But when I looked at the screen, I saw that Mom was calling.

Oh, crap. What now?

Tempted as I was to ignore her call, I decided to get it over with.

"You're not going to believe what I just found out!" Mom announced.

I didn't bother to respond. Mom didn't let me, anyway.

"Your cousin is going on the most outrageous trip," she told me.

My spirits lifted a little, thinking that maybe my cousin's news would be bad—which would be good news for me.

"She's going to the Antarctic," Mom said, as if my cousin may as well have been going to Mars.

There was no way this would play well with her relatives at the wedding. My mom's side of the family considered roughing it a stay at the Hyatt.

My spirits lifted further. Oh, yeah, here was one cousin I'd definitely outshine.

"And she's staying for the whole winter," Mom said. "At

some kind of a laboratory."

I got a weird feeling.

"You mean a research center?" I asked.

"Yes, I suppose. And she's on some sort of groundbreaking project," Mom said.

My weird feeling turned into a sick feeling.

"Supposedly they've found something frozen in the ice that can cure Alzheimer's," Mom said.

My cousin was going on a life-changing quest, to an exotic location, to find a cure for a major disease?

Oh, crap.

"She'll be there for months," Mom said. "And, of course, there's not one decent salon in the place. Can you imagine what her hair and nails will look like when she gets back? Isn't that the most bold and daring thing you've ever heard!"

I froze, unable to move or say anything—not that Mom noticed, because she blabbed on for a while and finally hung up.

Then it hit me.

Oh my God, I absolutely had to have that fabulous Domino clutch from Darby's boutique in time to show it off at the wedding. Somehow, some way, I had to talk her into jumping my order to the head of her production line.

When I got to Darby's shop I was relieved to see that an open sign replaced the one instructing customers to call for an appointment. I went inside. No one else was there, but I heard what I guessed was a sewing machine running in the workroom.

The wave of peacefulness washed over me, as it had the last time I was here. And I definitely needed it. I'd have to keep my wits about me if I was going to bob and weave my way through a conversation that would motivate Darby to ignore her other orders and make my Domino clutch right away.

Yeah, I know, it was kind of stinky of me, but come on, what choice did I have?

I spent a few minutes gazing at the Domino clutch on display, soaking in its beauty, imagining how awesome it would look at my cousin's wedding, then realized the sewing machine wasn't running.

"Hello?" I called.

A few seconds later, Darby peeked through the curtains on the workroom doorway.

"Hi, Haley," she said, smiling easily and nodding toward the Domino. "Come to visit your bag again?"

"I can't stay away," I admitted. "All your bags are absolutely beautiful."

"Thanks." She held the curtain back. "Want to see where the magic happens?"

"You bet," I said.

I stepped into the workroom and a tingling sensation swept over me as Darby showed me around the space, pointing out the bag she was working on, the new fabrics and notions she'd purchased, and a radical—and totally awesome—design she was considering.

"You have the coolest job," I said.

"It's not all fun," Darby said.

She pushed back a muslin sheet that covered a shelving unit. On it were about a dozen slightly worn and obviously used handbags and backpacks.

"I also do repair work," Darby said. "It's not glamorous, but it helps pay the bills."

The backpacks looked familiar. I stepped closer and turned one of the black ones around. On it was the KGE Model Agency logo.

"You repair these for KGE?" I asked.

"For the models," Darby said. "They bring them in all the time. The fabric is cheap so it's always ripping and fraying. I patch them back together as best I can, so their boss doesn't give them a hard time."

"Katrina," I mumbled. "That figures."

"She says they're all accountable for the backpacks so the models have to pay for the repairs themselves."

"Accountable, huh?" I asked.

At least now I knew what Katrina had been ranting about those times I'd heard her carrying on like a raving lunatic in the lobby.

"That's kind of crappy of her," I said.

"It is," Darby said. "Since the girls need their backpacks with them when they're working, I repair them as soon as they're dropped off."

I definitely needed to turn this conversation to something more pleasurable—and something that would convince Darby to make my Domino bag right away. Immediately, I came up with a plan.

"You remember I mentioned I was an event planner working on the fashion crawl?" I said. "I work for L.A. Affairs so I deal with a lot of stars and celebrities, Hollywood insiders. I know they would love your handbags. I could talk up your business, get you a lot more orders."

Darby shook her head. "No, but thanks."

"It's no trouble," I insisted. "Your bags are fantastic. I'd love to spread the word."

"No, really, it's okay. Honestly, I have more business than I can handle," Darby said. "I don't want to hire anybody to help because that's the point of my business—each bag is handmade by me. It's personal. Unique. I don't want that to change."

I was majorly disappointed but I understood what she was saying. After all, those were all the points I intended to use at the wedding to brag about my Domino clutch.

Still, I wasn't about to give up on finding a way to get my bag moved up in her production line. There had to be something I could do.

* * *

"Wow," Bella said.

We were standing in Holt's staring at a long row of empty shelves and clothing racks that had just been installed near the store entrance. I'd clocked in for my evening shift a few minutes ago and was on my way to tonight's assigned corner of Purgatory, the shoe department, when Bella flagged me down.

"It doesn't look wow-worthy to me," I told her.

"Me either," Bella said, "but that's what they're calling it. The wow aisle. It's supposed to be flashy and draw the customers over to look at whatever is displayed there."

"So what's being displayed?"

"Don't you ever pay attention in meetings?"

I didn't bother to answer and, really, Bella didn't seem to expect me to because she said, "Get this. The wow aisle is launching with the new spring clothing line."

"Oh my God ..."

"Yeah. I know," Bella said.

"What idiot in the marketing department came up with this idea?"

"I don't know," she said. "But I hope they thought to have paramedics standing by when the customers see those hideous clothes and stampede back out of the store."

"The collection is still under wraps in the stockroom," I said. "I can't bring myself to look."

"I wish I hadn't peeked. I'm still having nightmares," Bella said. "No way am I participating in that new contest."

"Oh, yeah, the customer service contest," I said. "I'd forgotten all about it."

"You're not going for it?" Bella asked and looked surprised, for some reason.

"Heck, no," I told her.

Bella gave me an I-know-you-too-well look, as only a best friend can, and said, "You really weren't paying attention in the meeting, were you."

Rita's face—with an I-can't-wait-to-ruin-your-night expression—appeared over the shelving unit next to us. Bella and I exchanged a see-you-later eyebrow bob, and I headed for the shoe department.

Something about trying on shoes made women lose their minds—I know because that's what happens to me—so the department looked as if hordes of looters had swept through on the eve of a zombie apocalypse. Boxes, lids, tissue paper—plus anything that would fit on a foot—were scattered in the aisles. To the untrained observer, this might look as if it created a great deal of work for the poor grunt of a sales clerk saddled with the job of clean up, but for me it meant I had a perfect excuse to ignore customers.

Moving at my usual I-can-stretch-this-out-until-closing pace, I focused my attention on boxing and shelving. Luckily, I didn't have to think too hard about the task so my brain was free to roam through more entertaining thoughts.

Finding a way to get Darby to make my Domino clutch in time for my cousin's wedding was big in my head, of course. I was confident I could come up with a way to get her to let me jump the line, then oh-so-casually drop by her boutique and spring it on her. All I had to do was come up with the brilliant idea.

But instead of conjuring up a desperately needed brilliant idea, my thoughts turned to Rayna's murder. Maybe it was seeing the KGE backpacks in Darby's shop—I still thought it was ultra crappy of Katrina to use cheap fabric for the bags and then force the models to pay for the repairs—or maybe there was another reason I suddenly focused on the image of the crime scene. I couldn't be sure. Something about finding Rayna's body seemed *off* to me, and I still couldn't pin down exactly what it was.

My cell phone vibrated in my back pocket. I shoved the boxes of shoes I was carrying onto an empty shelf—they didn't belong there, but oh well—and ducked into the stockroom.

I was mega-grateful for the interruption, and it hit me how dreadful it must have been for people back in the day when they were at work with nothing to do but actually *work*. How did they take care of their personal business, keep up with friends, and make plans for when they got off?

Standing among the shelving units filled with boxes of shoes, I pulled out my phone and saw that Marcie had texted me about plans for the weekend. See? Having a cell phone was essential to daily life now. Good thing I wasn't living back in the '80s—though I'm sure I could have totally pulled off the chunky jewelry, shoulder pads, and big hair—because no way could I run my life without my phone. And not just my personal life. I'd be lost without my phone at L.A. Affairs. In fact, I didn't know anyone who had a job that didn't rely on—

Wait. Hang on a minute.

Rayna's cell phone. I'd seen it lying next to her body at the foot of the stairs. At the time Clark had speculated that she was on her phone, not paying attention, and had fallen down the stairs. I hadn't given it another thought until now.

Oh my God, maybe Rayna had actually been talking to someone when she'd confronted her killer at the top of the stairs. Had she, perhaps, told that person who she'd run into? Named a name? Had whoever was on the other end thought their call had simply been dropped, and not realized what had actually happened? Was there someone out there who knew who had killed Rayna?

Then something else hit me.

This had to be the weird something's-not-right-here thoughts that had been rambling around in my head about finding Rayna, the thing that I hadn't been able to pinpoint.

Then yet another thing hit me.

Had the homicide detectives thought to check this out and identify the caller? Probably, I decided—detectives were really smart guys—which meant, of course, that it was possible for me to get the info.

I called Detective Shuman.

He didn't answer—which irritated me that he wasn't available to act on my oh-so-brilliant revelation—so I left a message asking him to call me.

I tucked my cell phone into my pocket and did a couple of fist pumps, confident that I was onto something. Rayna's murderer would be revealed in short order, the fashion crawl would therefore come off without a hitch, and I wouldn't lose my job at L.A. Affairs.

Do I totally rock, or what?

I was amped up by the I-know-this-will-work-out turn of events, which caused me to work faster, and thankfully, made my shift go by quicker. I punched out, grabbed my handbag—a fabulous Coach tote—from my locker, and beat everyone else out the front door into the Holt's-will-do-anything-to-save-a-buck poorly lit parking lot.

As I approached my car, I noticed another vehicle start up down the row. Headlights came on. It whipped out of the space and screeched to a halt, blocking my car.

The driver leaned across the seat and opened the passenger-side door.

"Get in," he told me.

I got in.

Chapter 11

It's like I always say—you never know when something good is going to happen to you and this was, wow, way better than good.

"What's the deal?" I asked.

Jack glanced at me as he drove through the Holt's parking lot. I couldn't always tell from his expression exactly what was on his mind—I'm sure he did that on purpose—so my thoughts ran wild thinking he was about to whisk me off on a wild, exotic getaway, or that he had a tough case to solve and couldn't possibly move forward without my help.

But, instead, Jack surprised me by throwing a half-grin my way and saying, "You worked two jobs today. I figured you could use a beer."

Not a getaway or a hot case, but I'd take it.

Jack drove to a bar a few miles away on Soledad Canyon Road and we went inside. It wasn't fancy, upscale, or trendy, which I appreciated since I was dressed in my Holt's I-look-crappy-to-match-this-crappy-place attire. Jack looked fantastic, of course, in black cargo pants and a navy blue shirt. The lighting was low, a TV over the bar was tuned to the Dodgers in extra innings, and the few people scattered around the place were chatting quietly.

We got a table in the corner. Jack sat with his back to the wall, like a gunslinger in an Old West saloon expecting trouble to walk through the bat-wing doors—which was way hot, of course. The waitress came over right away, greeted Jack by name—jeez, this guy knows *everybody*—and took our order, beer all round.

Despite Jack's effort to make his sudden appearance seem casual, I knew he wouldn't have shown up in the Holt's parking lot unless he had something significant to share with me—although I did appreciate the beer and could definitely use one—which made me slightly antsy, thinking there was a problem with the fashion crawl.

I was about to ask Jack what the heck had happened when he

asked, "Did you pick out a handbag?"

I remembered then that I'd run into Jack on the street outside Darby's boutique. While I really needed to know what was up with the crawl, talking about the Domino clutch was way cooler.

"Yes. Oh my God, look at this bag." I got out my cell phone and showed him the photo I'd taken. "It's the Domino. Isn't it gorgeous?"

Jack took his time studying the pic, then asked, "Are you taking it some place special?"

I groaned—but not in a good way. "My cousin's wedding."

Jack reeled back slightly and, really, I couldn't blame him. Family weddings had that effect on most everyone.

"I *want* to take it," I explained. "But the bag won't be ready in time. Darby sews each of them by hand so there's a waiting list. I don't know what I'm going to take to the wedding now. And, as if that weren't bad enough, I don't have a plus-one either."

Jack flinched and, again, I couldn't blame him. Single, unattached people were considered fair game by friends saddled with invitations to do-I-really-have-to-go-to-this-thing occasions, and constantly lived in fear of being dragged along under the guise of friendship—sort of like any guy who owned a pickup truck had to always be on guard against somebody asking for help moving.

No way would I ask Jack to suffer through my cousin's wedding—nobody wanted to deal with their own family, let alone somebody else's—so I decided this was a good time to change the subject.

"So what's up?" I asked.

Jack pulled a folded slip of paper from his shirt pocket and slid it across the table to me.

"The woman you were looking for," he told me.

I glanced at the note and saw contact information for Melody Case, the agent who'd left KGE.

"Thanks," I said. "Beer's on me."

"Forget it."

"Come on," I said. "I have to do something for you."

"You will."

A toe-curling, stomach-fluttering expression came over Jack's face.

—

"When I decide what I want, you'll know it," he told me.

Thank God he hadn't used his Barry White voice. I'm totally helpless against his Barry White voice. Still, every intelligent thought flew right out of my head—how could it not?

Luckily, the waitress showed up with our beer. I grabbed my mug, took three big swings, and tried desperately to think of something to say.

Nothing came to mind.

"I didn't find anything on that lawsuit you asked me to check into," Jack said.

What the heck was he talking about? Should I really be expected to think at a time like this?

I took another gulp of my beer and forced my brain to work. I realized he was talking about the upcoming trial involving one of the fashion designers that Rayna was supposed to testify for, one of my maybe-this-will-reveal-some-actual-evidence motives for her murder.

"It got dismissed?" I asked. "I guess it would, since a key witness had gotten murdered."

"It never existed," Jack told me.

Okay, that was weird.

I almost asked Jack if he was sure his information was reliable, but that would have been insulting and no way would I offend Jack. Besides, he knew a lot of people and had access to a lot of information, so I had no reason to doubt him. Still, I was surprised and a little weirded-out about the whole thing.

"Who told you about the lawsuit?" he asked.

"Somebody who works for KGE," I said. "For Katrina, actually. Her personal assistant, Libby. She said it was a hush-hush matter. Nobody was supposed to know about it."

"She must have misunderstood what was happening," Jack said.

Okay, that made sense. Libby hadn't struck me as being on top of everything—how could she when Katrina had her running in circles most of the time—so perhaps she wasn't clear on what Rayna had told her or she'd remembered it incorrectly. It could have happened.

Still, I felt kind of bad that I'd asked Jack to waste his time—and probably burn a favor—investigating a possible motive that had never actually existed. Then it hit me that I'd mentioned it to

Detective Shuman, too. Great. Now I looked like an idiot in front of both of them.

And, of course, that also meant that one of the avenues of investigation I'd counted on to find Rayna's killer no longer existed. Except for remembering the cell phone lying next to her body, I hadn't come up with anything new.

"We're still contending with the homeless who are living in some of the buildings you're using for the fashion crawl," Jack said.

Dealing with this displaced portion of the population was troubling and disturbing. My heart went out to all of those people whose lives had taken such a bad turn that they'd found themselves in this situation. It was a tough problem that a lot of government agencies and volunteers had been trying to fix for a long time, with no easy answers or permanent solutions.

"They won't leave?" I asked. "I know their circumstances are bad but, technically, isn't that trespassing?"

"They leave, but they come back," Jack said. "We'd need twenty-four hour security, and from what I'm hearing, a lot of the building owners won't go for it."

"It would be expensive," I agreed.

"Other owners are pushing hard to get them out, no matter what the cost."

"The crawl could lure big companies looking to relocate in North Hollywood," I said. "It would be a great opportunity for the owners to unload an empty, profit-draining property."

Jack said, "Some of the building owners are talking about legal action to clear out the homeless."

"Not good," I said and cringed, visualizing headlines splashed across newspapers, magazines, and the internet. "Taking legal action could turn the situation into a news story. Evicting the homeless for a fashion crawl? Nobody wants that kind of publicity."

"The issue will be resolved before the crawl," Jack said, "as discreetly as possible."

He made it sound like it was no big deal, but I couldn't let it go so easily. If the story blew up the internet and Twitter, then made its way to the mainstream media, the negative publicity could crush the crawl, devastate the sponsors, and wipe out all the work that had gone into the event so far—not to mention, of course, that L.A. Affairs would take a hit to their all-important reputation which might result in them blaming me, somehow, and firing me.

Jack must have read the my-life-could-plunge-into-a-death-spiral expression on my face because he said, "Relax. I'm handling it."

Most anyone else might have figured this was the best they could hope for, and while I did have complete faith in Jack and his hand-picked security team, this was a situation that wasn't completely under his control. No way was I going to sit around, think good thoughts, cross my fingers, and hope for the best.

That's not how I roll.

I was going to do everything in my power to make this fashion crawl a success. And since I didn't have any influence over the homeless, I figured the only thing left for me to do was find Rayna's murderer.

Luckily, I had a new place to look.

* * *

It was a Gucci day. Definitely a Gucci day.

Spotting an empty packing space at the curb along Coldwater Canyon Avenue, I whipped into it. Like I always say, you never know when something good is going to happen to you, and finding a vacant parking spot in Studio City without circling the block over and over, cutting someone off, or taking whatever you could find and hoping your car didn't get towed was definitely a good way to start my day.

My Gucci satchel helped, too, of course. Using my handbag superpower while standing in front of my closet this morning, I'd selected it to go with my navy blue business suit, which I totally rocked.

I'd gone by my office at L.A. Affairs just long enough to make sure the office manager saw that I was there—and to grab coffee and a chocolate doughnut from the breakroom—before I headed out. I had some venues and a couple of vendors to check on for several of the events I was handling, which was good cover for visiting—okay, ambushing—Melody Case at the address Jack had given me last night.

I got out of my Honda and headed down the block to the

apartment complex Melody lived in. The building was white stucco with arched doorways and a red tile roof, on a tree-lined, highly sought-after street that was walking distance from busy, upscale Ventura Boulevard.

The info Jack provided didn't mention whether Melody, after leaving the KGE agency, had gotten another job. I'd done an internet search on her, but hadn't come up with anything so I figured I would take a chance, and show up on her doorstep—besides, it was a good reason to stay away from the office longer.

I located her apartment on the first floor, and just as I reached for the bell, the door flew open.

I knew the woman standing in front of me was Melody because I'd seen her photo on the KGE website. She was probably early thirties, jet black hair cut in a chic bob, tall and shapely. She was dressed in jogging clothes.

Seeing me standing there she jumped back, startled.

"Sorry, I didn't mean to scare you," I said, and gave her my best I'm-really-a-nice-person grin.

She pulled buds from her ears. "I wasn't expecting anyone."

I introduced myself and presented my L.A. Affairs business card. She read it, and looked up at me.

"I don't need an event planned," she said, looking slightly suspicious now and maybe a little concerned because she stepped outside and pulled her door closed behind her.

"I know," I said. "I want to talk to you about the KGE Model Agency."

"No way."

She cut around me and jogged away.

Chapter 12

"Jeez, Melody," I called. "I'm wearing three inch pumps. You don't expect me to chase you, do you? Give me a break, will you?"

She ran a couple of more steps, then stopped and turned around. Obviously, she'd worn similar shoes herself, because she walked back to where I waited on the sidewalk.

"What's this about?" she asked.

I could see she wasn't happy about my intrusion, so I didn't bother trying to finesse anything.

"I'm the event planner for the fashion crawl," I told her. "KGE is a major sponsor. There's a potential problem, a huge one. Nobody at the agency is giving me the info I need, so I figured you would."

"I haven't worked there in nearly a month," Melody told me. "I don't know what kind of help I could be."

"One of their models was murdered."

Melody gasped. "Oh my God, I hadn't heard. Who was it?"

"Rayna Fuller."

Her shoulders slumped a little and she shook her head. "I worked with Rayna, handled her castings and bookings. And she was murdered? What happened?"

I gave her a few seconds to take it in—she seemed genuinely surprised and upset by the news—then explained about Rayna's fall and that the police were calling it a murder.

"It hasn't made the news yet, but if word gets out it could completely destroy the fashion crawl—plus, of course, whoever did this should be found and punished," I said. "The police aren't making any headway so I wanted to get your take on Rayna. Everybody says she was nice. But nice people don't usually get murdered. What did you think of her?"

Melody paused, seeming to collect her thoughts, then said, "I liked Rayna. She was always cheerful, sweet, thankful for whatever bookings I could find for her. She was nice. Really nice."

"But ...?"

She huffed and glanced away. I could tell she wanted to say something more but was reluctant, probably because Rayna was dead and who wants to speak ill of a young woman who'd been murdered?

While I appreciated Melody's hesitation, I didn't have all day to stand around.

"Something wasn't right about Rayna, was it?" I said. "Please, tell me. It could help find her killer."

"Okay," Melody said. "I sometimes got a weird vibe from her. Nothing I could really put my finger on, but I felt that I could never get to know her. Rayna always said and did the right things, yet it seemed like it was all a façade, like she was hiding who she really was or what she was really doing."

"You mean, she was desperate for work and was crazy-nice to you since you did the model bookings?"

"It was something deeper than that. I don't know. It was odd," Melody said. "I did try extra hard to find her work. I knew she was struggling financially. I sent her out on every casting I could. Once I even called Emerald."

"That's a clothing line?" I asked.

"Emerald Graffiti," she said. "They only do plus-size clothing. The company is massive so they use a lot of fit models, which means they book a lot of hours. Rayna's specs were perfect for them."

"But it didn't work out?"

"I called Chyna, off the record, of course—"

"Emerald does their fittings in China?" I asked.

"It's a person, not the country," Melody explained. "Chyna Baine. She's the senior tech designer at Emerald."

The name hopped around in my head, but didn't settle on a memory. I knew I'd heard it before, somewhere.

"At first Chyna was interested—they always need plus-size models," Melody said. "Until I gave her Rayna's name. Then she pulled back and said she'd check the schedule and let me know. I never heard from her. It made me think something was going on."

"Like what?" I asked.

"I'm not sure," Melody said, then shook her head. "I let the whole thing drop, since it nearly got me fired."

85

I could see this was a personal issue with Melody and probably had nothing to do with Rayna's death, but jeez, I couldn't ignore this huge, juicy chunk of gossip.

"What happened?" I asked, and managed to sound stunned and outraged, not simply nosey.

Melody grumbled under her breath for a few seconds, then said, "Katrina got wind of my call to Emerald. I don't know how, but she did. She threw an absolute fit that I'd contacted them. We're not supposed to do business with Emerald. Period. End of story."

Okay, I was confused.

"But you said they book tons of hours for plus-size models," I said. "That would mean major bucks for KGE, wouldn't it?"

"You bet. It's standard that any clothing design company who uses an agented model has to pay her agency an additional twenty percent of her hourly wage, on top of what they pay the model," Melody explained. "You want to hear something crappy?"

I always wanted to hear something crappy.

"KGE also takes fifteen percent out of what the models are left with," Melody told me.

"Wait a minute," I said. "You mean KGE collects twice for every booking?"

"Crappy, huh?" Melody said. "Most of the models are young, not the least bit business savvy. They sign the KGE contract without understanding what they're really agreeing to. By the time they figure it out, it's too late. They're locked in."

"That's mega-crappy," I said.

"Some of the models pick up bookings independently so they don't have to pay KGE," Melody said. "Can't say that I blame them."

"So where do Emerald Graffiti and you nearly getting fired fit into this situation with Rayna?" I asked.

"Emerald doesn't use agented models, just girls who work independently. I know Chyna pretty well, so I thought maybe I could sneak something by for Rayna's sake."

"That's what Katrina nearly fired you over?" I asked. "Because you tried to steer one of her models to Emerald Graffiti?"

"It was because of a lawsuit."

86

My now-we're-getting-somewhere invisible antennas shot up.

"I'd heard Rayna had gotten tangled up in a legal matter with one of the designers," I said.

Melody shook her head. "This lawsuit was several years ago, way before Rayna signed with KGE. Back then Emerald used agented models. There was a huge blow-up between KGE and Emerald over billing. It got really ugly. As a result, Katrina won't allow anyone to even say the name 'Emerald Graffiti' in the office, and Emerald went to an unagented-models-only policy."

"Wow, that must have been one heck of a blow-up," I said. "So you quit before Katrina could fire you?"

Melody shrugged. "Partly. But mostly it was because the agency was circling the drain. I wasn't going down with that sinking ship."

"What?" I might have said that kind of loud because, yeah, I was stunned.

The entire fashion crawl flashed in my head. KGE was a major sponsor. Huge commitments had been made, tons of money still needed to be spent, reputations were on the line— including mine. No way did I want to be known as the event planner who rode NoHo's inaugural fashion crawl into the ground.

"Katrina tried to cover up the problems at the agency, but I saw what was happening," Melody said. "First it was little things, like no more snacks in the breakroom. Then she started hounding us to get the models more work. She was more uptight than usual about expenses. The models started complaining that they weren't getting their paychecks on time. Then the employees who'd quit weren't being replaced."

"But I'd heard Katrina had other holdings, other income, not just the agency."

"I'd heard that, too. Whether it's actually true or not, I don't know, and I had no way of finding out," Melody said.

Maybe she didn't. But I did.

* * *

I'd swapped my fabulous Gucci bag for a Dooney & Bourke

barrel to better match my Holt's-wear when I'd stopped by my place to change after work, and was now headed across the parking lot for my evening shift. With a full six minutes left before I had to clock in, I dug out my cell phone and called Marcie. I'd tried to reach her earlier but my call had gone straight to her voicemail, which probably meant that, as usual, she'd let her battery run down and hadn't been able to find her charger.

"I couldn't find my charger," she said, as soon as she picked up. "Want to meet for dinner?"

"I'm slaving away in purgatory tonight," I said. "How about tomorrow night?"

"Sure," she said. "So what's up?"

"I need a favor."

"Okay. What?"

No hesitation, no reluctance, nothing. That's why Marcie's the best BFF on the entire planet.

"Have you still got that friend at the bank who can do a property search?" I asked.

"Oh my God, you're not involved in another murder, are you?"

Okay, now she was sounding a little less like a bestie.

Before she could shift into don't-get-involved mode, I said, "It's about the fashion crawl. I'm concerned that the major sponsor I've been working with may go belly-up and wreck everything."

Marcie was quiet for a minute then said, "Text me what you need."

"Thanks," I said. We firmed up our plans for tomorrow night, and ended the call.

I dashed off a quick message to her and headed inside the store to the breakroom, stowed my handbag in my locker, and fell in behind the other employees at the time clock. Rita stood by, marker in hand, ready to write my name on the white-board for being tardy. I gave her my middle-school snarky smile as I clocked in with two seconds to spare.

Not to be outdone, she barked, "I hope you're not thinking you're going to actually win one of the prizes in the contest."

Thanks to my competitive nature, my first thought was to enter the contest and win first prize, just to prove her wrong.

"You're on the schedule to take the test tonight," she said, waving her hand at a sign posted above the time clock. "But why bother?"

Some of the employees in the breakroom turned and stared. I ignored her.

"It's a contest about customer service," she said. "Customer service. Do you even know what that is, princess?"

Now everybody in the breakroom was staring.

"No, wait. I'd better clarify it for you," Rita said. "The contest is about *good* customer service."

Okay, now I really wanted to blast her with what I thought of that stupid contest, but I held back—yes, I know, that's totally unlike me, but I was kind of tired. Instead, I channeled my mom's beauty pageant queen I'm-better-than-you walk, and left the breakroom.

Still, I was fuming—and, I realized, I'd forgotten to look at the schedule to see which department I'd been assigned to tonight. No way was I going back in there for round two with Rita, so I headed across the store to walk off some of my irritation.

I spotted Sandy working in the children's clothing department—I hate that department—and she waved me over.

"Everybody's really going crazy about this new contest," she said, smiling and doing jazz hands.

Good grief, not this again.

"I can't believe you're not going for it," she told me. "I mean, winning a third-place prize wouldn't be all that great, but you'd love it."

"I doubt it."

"No, really, you would," she insisted.

I was in no mood. But Sandy was one of my Holt's BFFs and it wouldn't be right to take out my annoyance with Rita on her.

"So what's the third-place prize?" I asked, and actually sounded pleasant.

"Well, first prize is not exactly—"

"Just tell me about third place," I said.

Sandy's smile got wider and she said, "Third place is a one-hundred dollar gift card for Starbucks."

"What?" I'm pretty sure I said that too loud.

"Yeah!"

89

"Why didn't you tell me?" I screamed that.

"Isn't it great?" Sandy said. "Like I said, the first-place prize is—"

Everything she was saying turned into blah,blah,blah, which was just as well since I'd quit listening anyway.

Oh my God, a huge Starbucks gift card. I absolutely had to win it.

I was definitely taking that test tonight.

It's like I always say—you never know when something good is going to happen to you, and this was beyond good.

Then things got even better. I spotted Detective Shuman walking down the aisle toward me.

Wow, I was on a major roll tonight.

I left the children's department, caught his attention, and headed toward the stockroom. He followed me inside.

It was quiet, except for the music playing on the store's P.A. system. We had the place to ourselves.

Shuman had on his slightly mismatched cop-clothes. His shirt collar was open and his tie was pulled down. He looked tired. I figured he'd had a tough day—and when a homicide detective had a tough day, it was really tough.

Still, he gave me a smile. Nice.

"How did you know I was working tonight?" I asked.

His grin turned kind of crafty and he said, "I'm a detective, remember?"

I guess that meant he'd gone by my apartment and not seen my car, so he'd taken a chance and driven here. Not Miss-Marple-quality detective work, but I was glad he'd put in the effort and given my day a boost.

"I'm in the middle of something," Shuman said, his smile disappearing, "but I wanted to give you some info."

I figured he was on a case, and if he needed a short break, it must have been a bad one.

"Rayna Fuller wasn't a party in a lawsuit," Shuman said.

Jack had told me the same thing, and while I'd trusted his info, hearing it from Shuman left no doubt.

"Another dead end," I said. "I don't suppose anything new has come up? A clue? Suspect? Some evidence, maybe?"

Shuman shook his head. "Nothing."

Then I remembered my this-will-break-the-case awesome

idea that I'd wanted to ask him about, and said, "What's up with Rayna's cell phone? She must have had it in her hand when she tumbled down the stairs because I saw it lying next to her. Was she talking to someone?"

He grew still and I was pretty sure I saw his cop-brain engaging.

"I'll check into it," he said.

I'd hoped for a bigger this-will-break-the-case-and-you're-awesome response.

"Sorry to send you on a wild goose chase with the whole lawsuit thing," I said.

Shuman managed a small smile. "It was worth it."

I took that to mean stopping by to give me the info in person had brightened his day. Cool.

Still, I couldn't shake my troubling thoughts about the supposed lawsuit.

"I don't know why Libby gave me that info," I said. "I guess she was confused, or misinformed."

Shuman frowned, shifting into cop-mode again. "Or maybe she was deliberately lying."

I guess she could have been. But why?

Chapter 13

The fashion crawl was drawing closer—almost crunch-time—so it was imperative that I stayed on top of everything; no way could I leave any details for the last minute. I'd emailed Peri twice to finalize the menu for the dessert stations but hadn't heard back. I figured she was elbow-deep in problems since the agency was short-staffed, so I decided to stop by and see her in person.

A spot opened up in the lot outside of the KGE building so I whipped into it, then realized that the Paint Masters van was parked a couple of spaces over. Clark was still painting the office suite, apparently.

I'd put him on my mental maybe-he-did-it-even-though-I-have-no-evidence suspect list. He was still hovering around in the back of my mind for no real reason, except that he'd been evasive about his actions immediately prior to discovering Rayna's body at the foot of the steps. With no new info to go on in the investigation, I decided it was time to dig into his life. Maybe I'd get lucky and find out he was some sort of weirdo serial killer.

Digging my cell phone from my handbag—a take-me-seriously Burberry tote that paired perfectly with my black YSL suit—I googled Clark's name and got a lot of hits. Wow, this guy was everywhere.

I clicked through all the links, my spirits sagging with every site I hit. Clark didn't work for Paint Masters, he owned it. And not only that, he was an artist who'd done murals for most every city in Southern California, plus big name celebrities and billionaires.

He'd told me that the guy who was supposed to paint the office suite had a family problem so he'd taken the job, which meant he was also a really nice person.

Crap.

This left me with no choice but to mark Clark off my suspect list. Though why he'd been popping in and out of the office suite he was painting the day of the murder, supposedly waiting for someone to arrive, and claimed he didn't have his cell on him, I still didn't know—except that maybe he was one of those artsy people and everybody knows how weird they could be sometimes.

I left my car, but instead of heading for the KGE office, I looped around the building and headed for Darby's boutique. While paying a cordial visit to the soon-it-will-be-mine Domino clutch would give my day a boost, I had an ulterior motive for going there.

My cousin's wedding was getting bigger in my head with each day that passed, making it more and more imperative that I get my hands on the Domino. This morning when I'd walked into my office at L.A. Affairs, the perfect way to get Darby to make my clutch immediate had—wham—popped into my head. I intended to hit her with it this morning and, yeah, she'd be crazy to turn me down.

As I was mentally rehearsing my oh-so-clever ploy, my gaze locked in on the Starbucks across the street. The Holt's employee contest lit up my brain.

Normally, thoughts of Holt's would be a bad thing, but all I could think right now was how great it was going to be when I won the third-place prize and got my hands on the one-hundred dollar gift card from my favorite place on the planet.

I'd taken the test last night before my shift ended, twenty what-has-become-of-my-life minutes of reading and answering questions on a computer set up in the Holt's training room.

Finessing the test had been a bit tricky. No way did I want to do well enough to win the first- or second-place prize—whatever they were—and I didn't want to tank and end up with a crappy Holt's beach towel.

It had hit me then that getting third place wouldn't be so hard. The other employees would be going all-out for first or second and, really, since I'd drifted off through every training session—including my new-employee orientation—there was no chance I could do better than third, anyway.

My cell phone buzzed. I glanced at the ID screen and saw that Mom was calling.

Crap—just when I was feeling great about everything.

Then I thought—oh my God—maybe she'd tell me the wedding was off.

"You're not going to believe what your cousin has done," Mom exclaimed as soon as I answered. "It's the most amazing thing."

Obviously, the wedding was still on.

Damn.

"You know she and her husband, the neurosurgeon, just bought that beautiful historical mansion in Philadelphia that they're restoring," Mom said.

I had no idea which cousin she was talking about.

Mom didn't seem to notice.

"Guess what they found—an original Declaration of Independence," Mom said. "It was in the attic. They're in the process of authenticating it now and—"

I stopped listening.

I held the phone to my ear until Mom wound down, then hung up.

I mean, really, how was I supposed to compete with that? Oh my God, this wedding was going to be a complete nightmare for me, my worst fears realized in front of every relative on Mom's side of the family.

I drew in a big breath, gritted my teeth, and hardened my resolve. No way was I going to crash and burn in a flaming heap of humiliation at that wedding. I was getting that Domino clutch.

Somehow, I'd forced myself to calm down by the time I walked into Darby's shop. I spotted her waiting on a customer, a woman with super-short it's-gray-now-so-why-should-I-care hair, wearing a floral print dress and a crocheted shrug.

Darby's smile was frozen on her face, and I could see it wasn't going well. The woman peppered her with questions and didn't seem to like any of the answers—when you get old, it seems, you hate things for no good reason—then finally left without buying anything.

Darby heaved a small sigh of relief and asked, "Come to visit your bag again?"

"I can't stay away," I admitted.

Even though I'd planned a subtle run-up to my latest sure-fire attempt to get Darby to make my bag immediately, I ditched that idea and jumped right in.

"You know, I'm planning the fashion crawl," I said. "I can get you a kiosk in a prime location. I'd be happy to do it. It's no trouble."

Okay, it would be a lot of trouble—but well worth it.

"No, thanks anyway," Darby said. "I'm not showing at the crawl."

For a few seconds, I thought I hadn't heard her correctly.

"But your business is local," I said. "Why aren't you participating?"

"I won't be at this location much longer," Darby said. "The landlord is increasing the rent."

Jeez, you'd think that at hundreds of dollars a pop for a handbag, she could afford to shell out a little more every month.

Darby must have read my mind, somehow, because she said, "The building has major problems. All the tenants have complained, but the landlord refuses to fix anything. Honestly, I've had enough of it."

A thread of high-panic whipped though me.

"You're not going to quit making the bags, are you?"

"I'll continue with my business, but I'm going to do everything online," Darby said. "Don't worry. I'll get your bag to you on time, as promised."

"Or sooner?" I asked.

She gave me an indulgent smile. "Sorry, no sooner."

Damn.

"How much longer will you be in your shop?" I asked.

"Just until the end of the month," she said. "I'm trying to tie up loose ends before I go. You know, get all the bags picked up that I repaired, handle the appointments I've already scheduled. I want the transition to go as smoothly as possible."

"If something changes and you decide to participate in the fashion crawl, let me know," I said. "You design beautiful handbags. I'd be happy to help show them to the world."

Darby smiled and said, "Thanks."

I left the boutique feeling more than slightly bummed. Not only had my awesome plan gotten me no closer to having my Domino, Darby was actually leaving the area.

With a quick look at Starbucks across the street—it called my name, I swear—I knew a mocha frappuccino was the only thing that could really lift my spirits today. I decided to get my meeting with Peri over with, and treat myself.

As I rounded the building, I spotted Clark standing at the rear entrance, dressed in his rainbow-splattered white pants and shirt. I was about to stroll over and chat for a bit—I felt a lot better about him since I decided he hadn't murdered Rayna—when I saw an SUV roll up next to him. A woman got out and started yelling at him, waving a cell phone, and pointing to the rear seat of the vehicle.

Obviously, something major was going down.

Maybe I'd been wrong about Clark.

I eased closer. The woman was young, dressed in stretched-out sweats, no makeup, with her hair pulled back in what had probably started the day as a ponytail. She hovered by the back door of the SUV. Inside, I saw the top of an infant seat.

I didn't need intel from Jack or Shuman to understand what was going on here. She was Clark's wife, and she was mega-upset with him because he'd left his cell phone at home and she'd had to load up their new baby to bring it to him—again, I gathered, from the way she screamed at him.

I did an about-face and headed for the front entrance of the building. No way did I want to get too close to all that. But it did explain why, on the day of Rayna's murder, Clark had been yo-yoing from the office suite to the hallway.

My already low spirits plummeted further. I'd thought Clark was really good looking and, except for suspecting him of cold-blooded murder, I'd wondered if something might spark between us. But he was married—and not simply married, married with a new baby.

Oh, crap.

* * *

After work I met Marcie for dinner at the Cheesecake Factory located in the super-cool Galleria across the street from L.A. Affairs. It had definitely been a cheesecake-desperately-needed kind of day. I always said you never knew when something good was going to happen. Well, not to sound selfish, where was my something good? Where was my great mojo? Why did these crappy things keep happening?

"Okay, talk," Marcie said when we sat down in a booth. "You're upset. What's going on?"

The waitress stopped by and we ordered drinks—not only

was it a cheesecake night, but a beer night.

"That gorgeous Domino clutch I wanted to take to my cousin's wedding," I said. "I talked to Darby again, trying to entice her to make my bag right away, but it's still a no-go. She's adamant about keeping to her production schedule."

"But that's good," Marcie pointed out. "You can be sure she won't push your bag back to make one for someone else."

Marcie was right, of course.

Marcie was almost always right.

But no way did I want to hear anything reasonable or sensible at the moment.

"I've got one idea left to try and convince her," I said.

Marcie must have sensed a Thelma-and-Louise moment coming, because her expression darkened.

"What are you thinking?" she asked, as if a little afraid to hear my answer.

"Darby told me there's some big anniversary party happening in her family and she doesn't have anybody to take," I said.

Marcie held up her hand and said, "Don't go there."

"I'm going to find her a date."

"No."

"I know a lot of good-looking guys," I said.

"Don't do it."

"I know I can find somebody she'll like, who'll impress her family. All I have to do is—"

"Forget it, Haley." Marcie said it kind of loud, as only a BFF can. "Don't get involved in her personal life."

"But I need that handbag," I insisted.

"No, you don't," she said, sounding way too reasonable.

The waitress served our drinks and a basket of bread. I chugged some of my beer.

"Look," Marcie said. "You don't need a Domino clutch, or any other kind of bag, to prove you're worthy of attending your cousin's wedding. You're not giving yourself enough credit. You look great, you have a terrific job, and you're dating a handsome, successful man."

At any other event, that might have been enough. But not with my mom's family. Marcie had a great home life, so she didn't fully understand what I was up against. If I didn't soon come up with a way to outshine my high achieving cousins, I'd

97

have no choice but to fake my own death.

"Besides, what if you do find Darby a date and the whole thing goes sideways," Marcie said. "She might refuse to make your bag, cancel your order."

Yikes! I hadn't thought of that.

"Promise me you won't try to find her a date," Marcie said, then added, "Or do anything else to get her to make your bag sooner."

Jeez, having a best BFF was really irritating sometime—especially when I knew she was right.

"Okay," I said, which I think I kind of whined, but it was the best I could do.

Marcie was quiet for a moment then, thankfully, changed the subject.

"I want to hear everything that's going on with you and Liam," she said. "But first, let me give you this, before I forget."

Marcie dug in her tote—a terrific Fendi that looked awesome with her gray suit—and passed me several sheets of paper.

"The property search you asked for," she said. "So who's Katrina Granger, anyway?"

"She owns the KGE Model Agency, the fashion crawl's major sponsor," I said, glancing over the printout. "I heard that the agency is having financial—oh my God, did you look at this?"

"Impressive, huh?" Marcie said.

Listed were the addresses of six properties that Katrina owned. I could hardly believe my eyes.

"Two are residential," Marcia said. "The others are commercial."

The commercial properties were all located in North Hollywood. I looked closer at the addresses and realized three of them were being used for the fashion crawl. They were vacant buildings, part of the homeless situation that Jack and his security team were struggling with.

It didn't take an MBA to know that Katrina had a ton of money wrapped up in these properties, and was losing a ton of money on them every month. Was that why the model agency was cutting back on expenses and payroll, screwing over the employees, and taking a nosedive?

Money was one of the biggest motives for murder, and

Katrina seemed to be eyeball-deep in financial problems. It made me think that her situation was somehow linked to Rayna's murder.

I just had to figure out how.

Chapter 14

Just as I whipped my Honda into a parking space in the L.A. Affairs garage the next morning, my cell phone rang. Jeez, the day had barely started and somebody was making a call already? No way could something important have happened, not this early.

"Katrina is having a meltdown," Peri said when I answered.

It seemed to me that Katrina was always having a meltdown so I figured that whatever was up with her now was nothing of consequence. Still, Peri sounded majorly stressed, which was totally unlike her.

I immediately morphed into event planner superhero mode.

"What happened?" I asked.

I used my I-can-fix-any-problem voice because, when it came to staging events, I really could fix any problem.

I like to think of it as another of my superpowers.

"The fashion crawl is disintegrating," Peri told me. "Katrina wants to fire the security firm because of the homeless situation. She's re-thinking all of the menus. She wants to completely revamp the VIP reception. And if those things don't happen, she wants to move the entire event to Santa Monica."

Oh my God—*oh my God*—that crazy Katrina couldn't be serious.

Fortunately, I hadn't said that aloud, only thought it.

"I'll be right there," I told Peri, and hung up.

All kind of plans, backup plans, contingency plans, suggestions, and recommendations pounded in my head as I drove to North Hollywood. No way could I allow Katrina to make any of those changes this close to the event. It simply could not be done. Not now. Not with the crawl merely days away.

I swung into a parking space outside the KGE building, thoughts of how to save the crawl roaring in my head. I had to stay focused and be persuasive when I talked to Katrina. It would take all my event planner superpowers to pull this off.

As I got out of the car and headed for the rear entrance, my cell phone rang. Figuring it was Peri, probably having a major meltdown herself by now, I grabbed it from my handbag and answered.

"I got that info for you."

It was Detective Shuman.

I didn't pause, didn't slow down. I had no time for this. I didn't even know what the heck he was talking about, and I had to get upstairs to KGE before Katrina lost what was left of her mind and did something really outrageous, like cancel the crawl completely.

"The cell phone caller," Shuman said. "The person Rayna was talking to when she was murdered."

I stopped on the sidewalk.

"It was Chyna," he said. "It's a person, not—"

"—the country," I said.

My heartrate picked up a little.

"Yes, Chyna Baine," Shuman said. "You know her?"

"She's a senior tech designer at Emerald Graffiti," I said.

All of my thoughts spun in a different direction now, abandoning the fashion crawl and Katrina and her meltdown.

"Why was Rayna talking to her?" I asked.

"I don't know. Chyna hasn't been interviewed yet. She's at the factory where they make the clothes in, get this, China." Shuman was quiet for a few seconds, thinking cop-thoughts, probably, then asked, "Do you know why they were talking?"

"No," I said.

"Haley?" He was using his cop-voice now.

"No, really, I don't know," I told him.

"But you have an idea?" he asked, as if he could read my thoughts.

Maybe he could because bits of information were flying around in my head, trying to connect.

"Nothing definite, just random thoughts that don't fit together," I admitted.

"Call me if something clicks."

"I will," I mumbled.

But honestly, I wasn't paying much attention to Shuman. I ended the call, my brain buzzing.

Rayna had been on the verge of turning her life around thanks to Colleen's departure from the KGE agency and only Ivy standing in the way of her taking over Colleen's long, lucrative list of clients. What a thrill Rayna must have felt, after eking by on the few fit modeling jobs that were available and settling for what amounted to crumbs, to suddenly know things were on the verge of turning around for her big-time at KGE.

So why had she been on the phone with Chyna?

Emerald Graffiti didn't use agented models, only girls who worked independently. Rayna had no reason to talk to Chyna. Unless, of course, Rayna was planning to quit KGE—but why do that, and give up all the other clients the agency could set her up with?

Still, there had to be a reason, something I'd missed. Since finding Rayna's body I'd felt like there was a loose end dangling that I couldn't identify. I'd thought it was her cell phone, but—

Wait. Hang on.

Rayna's backpack. Oh my God, her backpack.

A major lightbulb lit up my brain.

Her KGE-issued backpack wasn't with her at the foot of the staircase. That's what had seemed *off* about the crime scene. Oh my God, how could I have missed that?

Okay, I had to get my hands on that backpack. Maybe I could find something inside it that would indicate what was up with Rayna and Emerald Graffiti, and lead to her murderer.

Of course, the homicide detectives might have found it among Rayna's personal effects in her car or apartment. If so, they would have seen any evidence there that would have indicated who killed her, and closed the case by now.

But nobody had been arrested, and I doubted the detectives knew enough about fit modeling to realize Rayna should have had the backpack with her, and make it a priority.

So where would it be?

From what I'd seen, the models always had their backpacks with them.

Had her murderer taken it? That would mean it held incriminating evidence and, surely, was long gone by now. But if not—

Then it hit me.

I'd seen some KGE backpacks in Darby's workroom, left there for repair. Could Rayna's bag be there?

I hustled over to Darby's shop and went inside. Luckily, no customers were there. I spotted her in the workroom.

"Just can't get enough of that Domino clutch, huh?" she said, and walked over.

"You know me pretty well," I said, and managed a small laugh.

Mentally, I'd already shifted into private-detective-wannbe mode. I had to play it cool now, play it smart. I was desperate to find out if Rayna's backpack was here and get my hands on it— but I had to do it without looking like I was desperate, of course.

Oh my God, why hadn't I asked Jack to come along? We'd be so awesome together on a covert op.

"I was on my way to KGE to handle a couple of things for the fashion crawl," I said, pleased that I sounded casual. "I remembered you'd said you were trying to tie up loose ends so you could close your shop, and I know you have backpacks from the KGE models here for repair. I'll be happy to drop them off."

Darby hesitated, apparently feeling uncomfortable, and rightly so, about handing over someone else's property to me. A few seconds dragged by, just enough that I was seriously contemplating grabbing the backpacks and taking off.

"Well, okay," Darby finally said.

She stepped into the workroom, then reappeared a few seconds later with a backpack, and passed it to me.

"This is the only one left," she said. "The others were picked up already."

I glanced at the repair tag looped around one of the straps. Rayna's name was on it.

It took everything I had not to do an I'm-awesome fist pump.

"The models always want them back the same day, since they never know when they'll be called for a fitting," Darby said. "I don't know why this model hasn't come for hers."

I saw no reason to mention that the backpack's owner was dead.

"Thanks for taking care of this, Haley."

"Glad to help," I said, then waved and left the shop.

I had to go through Rayna's backpack immediately, and I had to do it some place where nobody would see me. I slung it over my shoulder and headed toward the KGE building, just in case Darby was watching.

Inside, the old guy security guard gave me major stink-eye as I crossed the lobby. I ignored him and walked down the hallway.

As I approached the rear doors, I smelled paint and figured Clark was still working. I dashed into the ladies restroom, relieved to see that no one else was in there. I locked myself in a stall.

I hung the backpack on the hook on the back of the door. It was surprisingly heavy. Models, apparently, had to haul a lot of stuff around with them to do their fittings.

I wondered why Rayna had left it all inside the bag when she'd dropped it off. Then I remembered Darby saying that she made the KGE models a priority, and repaired them right away. I imagined Rayna dropping off her backpack—intending to return in a few minutes—then heading for KGE, going up the stairs, and confronting whoever had pushed her to her death.

Not a great picture. I forced it out of my head.

I unzipped the main compartment and peeked inside. It was stuffed with shapewear, black tank tops and leggings, and four pairs of shoes each with a different heel-height.

It made me sad—and slightly creeped out—seeing things that had belonged to Rayna when she was alive.

It hit me then that if there really was some vital evidence in the backpack, the police might need it for evidence and now my fingerprints and DNA were all over it. Oops. Guess I should have thought of that sooner.

Well, too late now. Besides, there might be nothing of any importance inside, and I didn't want to look like an idiot over the whole thing if it turned out to be another dead end.

I closed the compartment and opened the smaller one on the front of the backpack. I peered inside and—bingo—I spotted a book of vouchers. I pulled it out.

It was the size of a hardcover novel. The pages were sectioned off in sets of threes, with each page a different color—white, which was the original, pink that was designated for the designer, and a yellow page which stayed in the book.

Each voucher had been completed by Rayna, indicating what designer she'd worked for, the date, her hourly rate and the number of hours she'd spent at the fitting. KGE's logo and address were on each page.

Flipping through the vouchers, I saw that Rayna's last fitting had been a week ago. Prior to that, she'd worked sporadically, an hour here, two hours there, for the last several months, confirming what I already knew.

Not exactly the hot evidence I'd hoped for.

Crap.

I dug deeper into the compartment and pulled out a handful of papers. Receipts, mostly, from fast-food restaurants where Rayna must have stopped to eat, and from Wal-Mart where she'd purchased two new bras. There was a coupon for a discount on an oil change, her cell phone bill, and a stack of blank invoices.

Invoices? What the heck?

I looked them over and saw that they were designed to be filled out with the same information as the KGE vouchers, but in the corner was a logo that featured a measuring tape and scissors, and Rayna's name, address, and phone number.

Some of the random thoughts that had zipped around my brain, connected.

What if Rayna hadn't been content with the few modeling opportunities KGE sent her way? What if, all along, she'd been working independently, billing the designers directly, and keeping it a secret from KGE? Was that why she'd been on her cell phone with Chyna Baine at Emerald Graffiti?

KGE was having financial trouble. Losing Rayna's income would be one more blow. What if KGE had found out what she was doing?

Was it a motive for someone to resort to murder?

I ran down my mental list of suspects at KGE.

First, there was Ivy. With Rayna out of the way, all of Colleen's clients would go to her. But what did that have to do with Rayna working independently? I didn't see a connection.

I'd wondered about Peri and Libby. Both of them had been out of the office that day during the time Rayna had been murdered. They had opportunity. But what about a motive? Would either of them have pushed Rayna down the stairs because she worked independently?

I thought about Peri. In her position she, like Melody, must have noticed, or at least suspected, the agency was in financial trouble. How would she feel about Rayna deserting KGE in its time of need?

And Libby? Her income came directly from Katrina, not KGE. So why would she care that Rayna's actions impacted the agency?

Now I wondered about Katrina. She'd been out of the office

during the time of Rayna's murder. I'd wondered if her financial problems were somehow linked to Rayna's death. Since I hadn't had any real evidence, I hadn't considered Katrina a suspect.

I did now.

Of everyone at the agency, Katrina had the most to lose by Rayna going independent. Plus, she hated everything to do with Emerald Graffiti. Had she somehow found out that Rayna was working for them, confronted her on the stairs, totally lost it, and pushed her down?

I could see Katrina going bat-crazy, no problem. But murdering Rayna? Yes, she could have done that.

Yet it seemed to me that confronting Rayna and pushing her down the stairs was an act that went deeper than dislike for a design company and the loss of the agency's income from her fittings.

My thoughts cycled back through my suspect list.

Which of them had something more at stake in this whole thing? Something beyond the obvious. A motive that—

My brain made the jump to light speed and I *knew*.

I yanked out my cell phone and called Detective Shuman. His voicemail picked up and I said, "I know who murdered Rayna."

Chapter 15

I shoved everything into Rayna's backpack, grabbed it, and hurried out of the restroom. When I'd spoken with Peri earlier, she'd told me Katrina was in the KGE office. I doubted she'd leave, knowing I was on the way. I had to get up there right away—but not to talk about the fashion crawl.

As I dashed up the staircase, I heard the click of heels ahead of me. Rounding the curve I spotted Libby nearing the top, balancing a take-out tray in each hand, one holding large drink cups, the other piled high with food wrapped in paper. Her KGE backpack hung over one shoulder.

"Libby?" I called.

She didn't stop, though I was sure she'd heard me.

"Libby!"

I turned on the speed and reached the top of the stairs as she did, then stepped in front of her to get her to stop.

"Hey, Libby, what's the rush?" I asked and managed to sound friendly and casual, though my heart was racing—but not from climbing the stairs.

"Oh, Haley, hi," she said, trying to skirt around me. "I've got to go."

I dodged to the right, cutting her off and said, "I need to talk to you."

"I can't. I really can't. Not now." She gestured to the two take-out trays with her chin. "Katrina is waiting for this."

I knew that, with Katrina in the throes of a major meltdown, she was probably being more demanding than usual.

Libby moved to the left. I blocked her again. No way would I let her get past me.

"I have news for Katrina," I told her, using my this-is-something-great voice.

Libby paused and gave me a suspicious look. "What sort of news?"

"Good news," I told her, and made it sound cheerful.

She glanced down the hallway toward the KGE office, then

looked at me again.

"I know Katrina is having a rough day," I said. "So I thought you'd like to tell her yourself."

Libby's expression brightened slightly. Surely, she'd be thankful that Katrina received some good news right now, and delivering it herself would be a real plus.

"Okay, what is it?" she asked.

A cell phone rang. She glanced at her KGE backpack, and I could see her anxiety spin up again, which told me that it was probably Katrina calling, wanting to know where Libby was and why she hadn't brought her food yet.

I said, "I found Rayna's backpack."

I held it up. Libby gasped softly. Color rose in her cheeks.

"I know Katrina is big on everyone being accountable for their backpack," I said. "So you can tell her it's been located."

Libby's cell phone rang again. This time she didn't move, just stood there staring at the backpack.

"And more good news," I told her. "You know that lawsuit you told me about, the one that involved Rayna that you said might have been the reason she was murdered?"

Libby looked at me now. The pink in her cheeks drained away.

"I found out there never was a lawsuit," I said.

I guessed that Libby had invented the lawsuit story to throw suspicion onto someone outside the KGE agency, and conjure up some misdirection and a mysterious suspect. I had to hand it to her, it had worked for a while.

"But you already knew that, didn't you?" I told her.

Libby looked down the hallway again. "I have to go."

She tried to get around me, but I stepped in front of her.

"You made it up, didn't you," I said. "You wanted it to seem like there was another motive for Rayna's death."

"No, no, I ..."

"You saw Rayna that day," I said. "Here, on the stairs."

I was winging it now, taking my best guess at what had happened.

"She was on her phone," I said. "You overheard her conversation. You knew she was talking to Chyna at Emerald Graffiti."

Libby shifted back and forth, struggling with the take-out

trays. "Yes, okay, yes. I heard her on the phone. But—"

"You realized that Rayna was working independently," I said. "You knew that she would get all of Colleen's clients and then she'd turn her back on KGE, and cut the agency out of their commission."

A flash of anger crossed Libby's face. I knew I'd guessed correctly.

"That money belonged to the agency," Libby insisted. "Rayna had no right to go independent with those clients. I couldn't believe she would betray Katrina like that, and be so disloyal to her."

At the heart of the screwball relationship between Libby and Katrina was Libby's loyalty to her. I couldn't really fault her for it—to a point.

"But Rayna didn't see it that way," I said. "She didn't think there was anything wrong with what she was doing."

"You wouldn't believe the awful things she said about Katrina." Libby's emotions amped up, her anger rising. "She said that everybody at the agency hated Katrina. They called her awful names behind her back. She claimed that Katrina could have done more to get clients for her so she wouldn't have to do without things, waiting for the fit modeling to take off."

"Rayna's life was rough," I told her. "Maybe Katrina could have done more."

"Katrina is a wonderful person," Libby insisted. "If it hadn't been for her, I'd have been forced to move back to that dreadful little town, and work at some horrible place, and listen to everybody's I-told-you-so. I couldn't believe people were saying those terrible things about Katrina, and that Rayna was trying to screw the agency out of money."

"So you confronted Rayna," I said and gestured to the staircase. "Here. On the steps."

"I was going to show Katrina what she was doing," Libby declared. "I was going to let her see what Rayna was up to."

The whole thing came clear to me then.

"So you grabbed for her cell phone?" I said.

"I only wanted to show it to Katrina. I didn't mean for—"

"Libby!"

We both spun around and spotted Katrina barreling toward us.

"Oh my God," Libby moaned.

"Libby! Libby!"

"I'm sorry, Katrina. I'm sorry, I'm sorry, I'm sorry."

Libby rushed forward just as I turned, and we bumped into each other. One of the take-out trays flew into the air. It hit with a splash as the four drink cups burst open and soda drenched the floor and the stairs.

Libby screamed. She dropped the sandwich tray, then screamed again.

"Oh my God! I'm so sorry! I'm so sorry!"

Katrina butted between us, stepped in the soda, and slid forward. She teetered on the top step for a second before Libby grabbed her arm. I lunged for them, but I was too late. Both of them tumbled down the stairs.

Oh, crap.

* * *

"What's wrong with these people?" Bella mumbled.

"I think it's great," Sandy insisted. "Don't you, Haley?"

I looked again at the dozens of chairs set up near the Holt's entrance, filled with customers who were anxious—or, more likely, had nothing better to do on a Friday evening—to see the new spring clothing line make its debut on the stage and runway that had been set up. A curtain shielded the girls Holt's had hired to model the fashions for the grand reveal—or, probably, to keep the audience from bolting if they got a look at the clothes before the show started.

"I'm with Bella on this one," I told her.

When I'd reported for my shift a few minutes ago, I summoned the courage to look at the so-called collection. It was stunning—but not in a good way.

It included bandana-print dresses in purple, orange, and teal; sleeveless dresses adorned with poppies, daffodils, and daisies; lounge dresses with gathers in all the wrong places; embroidered and appliquéd caftans with what-were-they-thinking side splits; and a three-tiered crinkle-cotton dress with, for no apparent reason, a bunny on the front.

There were many other garments but after seeing those, I'd had to turn away—and that's saying something after what I'd seen at KGE yesterday.

I doubted the image of Katrina and Libby, limbs entangled, careening down the staircase, would ever disappear completely from my mind, nor would the sight of their crumpled and twisted bodies at the foot of the stairs. I'd called 9-1-1 and the paramedics had gotten there in minutes. The police followed shortly.

The old guy security guard—spying on me, I'm sure—had been at the other end of the hallway and saw Katrina slip in the soda, causing her and Libby to tumble down the stairs. I think it irked him to have to tell the police that he'd witnessed the accident and that I was in no way at fault.

"The best part is," Sandy said, "now we get to find out who won the customer service contest. Jeanette is going to announce all the winners before the fashion show starts."

My spirits lifted a little. After what I'd been through lately, I figured I was somehow owed the third-place Starbucks gift card prize.

"Here comes Jeanette," Bella said.

She was headed toward us down the main aisle wearing a mustard yellow mohair skirt and jacket.

She looked like a blonde Big Foot.

"Lord have mercy," Bella mumbled. "That's from the new spring collection."

Now I was doubly glad I hadn't looked at the entire line.

No way did I want to be too close to Jeanette's outfit—just in case fashion cooties actually existed—so I eased away down one of the aisles. As I was about to duck behind a display of who's-big-idea-was-this blouse-vest combos, I caught sight of Detective Shuman entering the store.

I knew he wasn't there to shop.

He saw me right away and walked over.

"You doing okay?" he asked.

Even though he still wore his cop-clothes, he sounded like a friend. I couldn't help smiling, especially after the day I'd had at L.A. Affairs.

I'd been on the phone constantly, juggling calls from vendors, the caterer, and reps for the VIPs demanding to know if the fashion crawl was going forward. News surrounding Katrina, the major sponsor, word of Rayna's murder that had somehow leaked, plus the problem with the homeless had everybody in a near panic. I'd left the office with a headache and no definite word on the crawl—but it didn't look good.

"I still have some ugly pictures in my head, but they'll fade," I said. "Have you heard anything new?"

Shuman nodded and said, "Katrina will make it, but her recovery and rehab will be a long one. Two broken legs, along with her other injuries, won't be easy to come back from."

That, of course, meant an uncertain future for KGE. Katrina was in deep financial trouble. She'd bet everything on the fashion crawl, thinking she could sell her vacant, money-draining buildings or, at least, find some tenants. It seemed that gamble might take the model agency down with it.

"And Libby?" I asked.

"Another few days in the hospital and she'll be discharged."

"And face murder charges," I said.

Libby had put up with a lot—a pittance of a salary that forced her to wear cheap clothes and steal food from the office fridge, all because of Katrina.

"Maybe not," Shuman said.

"What?"

"The detectives on the case interviewed her this morning," Shuman said. "She's denying everything."

Okay, that ticked me off.

"But she confessed," I told him. "She's guilty. Rayna fell down those stairs because of her. She told me everything that happened."

"It's your word against hers."

Now I was really ticked off.

"You believe me, don't you?" I asked.

"Of course," he told me. "But unless some evidence is found that implicates her, it's not looking good."

I huffed, totally out of sorts now. It wasn't right that Libby had caused Rayna's death—and might walk away as if nothing had happened.

"The detectives can't find any evidence?" I demanded. "Nothing?"

Shuman gave me a tiny cop-grin. "There's a partial fingerprint on Rayna's cell phone. The lab hadn't been able to identify it. Now we have a suspect to match it to."

Libby had told me she'd tried to get the cell phone away from Rayna so she could show it to Katrina. I knew that partial print would be hers.

"Okay," I said. "I feel better about the whole thing now."

Shuman glanced at his watch and a different kind of grin pulled at his lips.

"I've got to run," he said, and walked away.

Obviously, he had a date with Brittany tonight. And, yes, of course I was happy for him, but it was Friday night and here I was stuck working in Holt's.

Damn.

The noise from the audience awaiting the fashion show diminished slightly and I saw Jeanette climbing onto the stage.

If ever I needed something good to happen to me, it was now. I absolutely had to get third place in the customer service contest, and get that Starbucks gift card. Things had to get better.

Then my night got worse.

My cell phone vibrated in my back pocket. It was Mom.

"It's the most fabulous news yet," she declared when I answered.

Jeez, what could another one of my cousins have done that was more fabulous than the news Mom had already shared with me?

Nothing, I decided. There couldn't possibly be anything grander that Mom could report. This day was not going to get any worse.

"You know your cousin who took that photography class on a whim?" Mom asked.

I had no idea what she was talking about.

"Well, she's a natural. Sought after by everyone," Mom said. "And guess what? She's been invited to Buckingham Palace to photograph little Prince George and Princess Charlotte."

I hung up.

Sandy rushed over and grabbed my arm. "Hey, come on. Jeanette's about to announce the winners of the customer service contest."

Thank God, something good.

We wormed our way through the crowd that surrounded the stage. Employees were gathered in the aisles along with customers who hadn't gotten a seat. Jeanette was explaining the

---

113

contest to the audience.

"I tried really hard on the test," Sandy whispered. "I hope I win second place."

"Yeah?" I said. "What's the second place prize?"

Bella raised an eyebrow at me. "You mean you really don't know?"

"I'm shooting for third," I told her.

Bella just shook her head.

I got a weird feeling.

"And now," Jeanette said, "I'm pleased to announce the winner of the first annual Holt's customer service contest."

Sandy held out crossed-fingers on both hands and whispered, "But if I win first place, it will be okay. I'll give it to my grandma."

My weird feeling got weirder.

"And the first place winner is…" Jeanette drew an envelope from her jacket pocket and made a show of prying it open. "Haley Randolph!"

Applause broke out. Everybody turned and stared at me.

Oh my God, what had just happened? I'd won first place? *First place?*

Was this my worst nightmare come true? I actually *knew* something about Holt's customer service?

And not only that, but I knew more about it than anyone else in the store?

"Come on up here, Haley," Jeanette called, smiling and waving me over.

I couldn't move.

"She's clearly overwhelmed," Jeanette said to the audience. "So I'll let her absorb her big win. It's really exciting."

"Sorry, Haley," Sandy mumbled.

Bella shook her head sorrowfully.

"Because," Jeanette said, "the first place prize that Haley has just won is our entire new spring collection!"

Oh, crap.

The End

Dear Reader,

There's more mystery out there! If you enjoyed this novella, check out the other books in my Haley Randolph series. You might also like my Dana Mackenzie series featuring an amateur sleuth who takes on the faceless corporation she works for while solving murders.

Would you like to add a little romance to your life? I also write historical romance novels under the name Judith Stacy. Get the latest at JudithStacy.com.

More information is available at DorothyHowellNovels.com where you can sign up for my newsletter, and there's always a giveaway going on. Join the fun on my Facebook page Dorothy Howell Novels, and follow me on Twitter @DHowellNovels.

Thanks for adding my books to your library and recommending me to your friends and family.

Happy reading!

Dorothy

Here's a sneak peek ...

DUFFEL BAGS AND DROWNINGS

By

Dorothy Howell

Here's a sneak peek at *Duffel Bags and Drownings*, another Haley Randolph novella.

Chapter One

"Something major is going down," Kyla murmured. "Have you heard anything?"

I hadn't but, of course, I wanted to.

"What's up?" I asked, filling my cup from the giant coffee maker on the counter.

We were squeezed into the breakroom of L.A. Affairs, the event planning company where we both worked as assistant planners, along with a dozen or so other employees all intent on delaying the start of our work day by spending an inordinate amount of time chatting about what we'd done the night before, what we planned to do today, and how we were going to get out of most of it—or maybe that was just me.

Kayla glanced around, then whispered, "Priscilla stopped Edie in the hallway."

Kayla--tall, dark haired, and about my age—had worked here longer that I had, so no way would I completely dismiss her warning. Still, the office manager stopping the head of H.R. in the hallway first thing in the morning, while troubling, was no reason to panic—especially before I'd had my first cup of breakroom-stalling-to-get-to-work coffee.

"They were whispering," Kayla said.

Okay, whispering in the hallway definitely amped things up. But, again, no need to panic. I, Haley Randolph, with my long pageant legs stretching me to an enviable five-foot-nine, my doesn't-it-make-me-look-smart dark hair, and my I'm-staring-down-25-and-not-panicking outlook on life, had been through this sort of thing before and knew it could mean absolutely nothing.

In the past few years I'd worked more than my share of jobs: life guard, receptionist, file clerk, and two weeks at a pet store. Add to that a bang-up job in the accounting department of the prestigious we-could-take-over-the-world Pike Warner law firm that could have worked out well for me if it hadn't been for that whole administration-leave-investigation-pending thing—long story. I'd landed at yet another fabulous company—another long story—where things hadn't worked out exactly as I'd hoped—none of which was my fault, of course.

The only job I'd managed to hold onto was a crappy part-time sales clerk position at the equally crappy Holt's Department Store which I intended to ditch—complete with the take-this-job-and-shove-it speech I'd rehearsed since my second day of employment there and the series of Olympic caliber cartwheels and backflips I intended to execute on the way out of their front door—as soon as my probation was up at L.A. Affairs.

The office was located in a high rise at Sepulveda and Ventura Boulevards in the upscale area of Sherman Oaks, not far from Los Angeles, amid other office buildings, banks, apartment complexes, and the terrific shops and restaurants just across the street at the Sherman Oaks Galleria. L.A. Affairs prided itself for its reputation as event planners to the stars, catering to upscale clients, the rich and famous, the power brokers and insiders of Los Angeles and Hollywood—plus anyone else who could afford our astronomical fees.

"It could be nothing," I said, emptying a packet of sugar into my coffee.

"Or it could be *something*," Kayla said, as she poured herself a cup. She gave me a quick nod over her shoulder. "Listen."

I noticed then that the early morning chatter in the breakroom was more subdued than usual. Not a good sign.

I dumped two more sugars into my cup.

Eve, another assistant planner, wormed her way between Kayla and me. Eve was a petite red head who was a few years older than me. She was a huge gossip so, of course, I'd become her BFF right away.

"Oh my God, something's up," Eve said, as she fumbled to fill her coffee cup. "Something big."

Kayla and I immediately leaned closer.

"What have you heard?" Kayla whispered.

"Nothing," Eve told us. "It's what I *saw*."

Kayla and I exchanged a this-is-definitely-something-major eyebrow bob.

"Priscilla and Edie were whispering in the hallway," Eve said. She paused, indicating the worst part of her story was about to be revealed, and said, "Then they went into Edie's office."

Oh my God. Kayla had been right. Something major was

definitely going down. I grabbed two more sugar packets and dumped them into my coffee.

"And," Eve announced, holding Kayla and I both in but-wait-there's-more suspense, "they closed the door."

Oh, yeah. This was bad, all right.

"Do you think they're going to lay someone off?" Kayla asked.

"Or fire someone," Eve said. "Maybe more than one person."

"Several people?" Kayla asked, shaking her head. "Who?"

Kayla and Eve both turned to me, and I got an all-too-familiar sick feeling in my belly. I'd been one of the last people hired at L.A. Affairs. Did that mean I'd be one of the first to go?

"Maybe they'll fire Vanessa," I said, and tried for a this-could-work-out-great smile.

Vanessa Lord was the senior planner I was assigned to—though we almost never spoke. She hated me, and I hated her back, of course. Vanessa brought the biggest clients to the firm which made her the biggest bitch in the firm, unfortunately.

"They'll never let Vanessa go," Kayla said. She managed a small smile. "But we can always hope."

"Keep your eyes open and your heads down today," Eve advised and left.

"Let me know if you hear anything," Kayla said, as she grabbed her coffee and headed out of the breakroom.

I topped off my cup with a generous amount of French vanilla creamer befitting the stress of the morning, and follower her out. In the hallway, I saw that the door to Edie's office was still closed. Not a good sign. I paused as I passed by—which was kind of bad of me, I know—and leaned closer. I heard murmurs but nothing specific—like my name being bandied about—so I went to my office.

I loved my office, my private sanctuary. It had a neutral desk, chair, bookcase, and credenza, and was accented with vibrant shades of blues and yellows. My favorite part was the large window that gave me a fabulous view of the Galleria across the street, and the surrounding area.

I had plenty of work to do, all sorts of events that I was in various stages of planning, but no way could I face them right now, not with this whole somebody-could-get-the-axe-today-and-it-could-be-me thing hanging over my head.

I walked to the window and looked down at the traffic creeping along the crowded streets, and the people rushing to get wherever they were going, and sipped my coffee. I had to admit to myself that this was an occasion when still having an official boyfriend to talk to would be good.

Ty Cameron was my last official boyfriend. He was absolutely gorgeous, super smart, organized, competent and professional, the fifth generation of his family to run the chain of Holt's Department Stores. If we were still together I could call him, talk this over, and he'd make me feel better—if he wasn't in a meeting, or on an international conference call, or had time to talk, of course.

We'd broken up for obvious reasons.

I sipped my coffee and thought about calling my best friend Marcie Hanover. She worked at a bank in downtown Los Angeles and was always available to discuss a problem, a fabulous new handbag I'd seen, or just about anything, as a BFF would.

But this didn't seem like a good time to call her.

It seemed like a good time to leave.

No way did I want to be around when Edie's office door opened, she and Priscilla walked out with personnel folders in their hands—possibly one with my name on it—and started calling people in.

I got my handbag—a terrific Chanel bag that perfectly accessorized my awesome navy blue business suit—grabbed an event portfolio, and left.

* * *

I got my Honda from the parking garage and headed west on Ventura Boulevard toward Encino. Traffic wasn't bad, considering, so it didn't take long before I reached the shopping center where Cady Faye Catering, my excuse to get out of the office, was located.

As I made the left turn into their parking lot, a black Land Rover pulled out of the driveway and turned right. I caught a glimpse of the driver. Oh my God, it was Jack Bishop. I nearly ran up on the curb.

Jack Bishop was a private detective, the hottest hottie in P.I. hot-land. Tall, dark haired, rugged build, and really good looking. I'd helped him out on some of his cases and he'd returned the favor a few times—strictly professional, of course.

For a couple of seconds I considered doing a whip-around and following Jack—just to be sociable, of course—but it was a total high school move and I couldn't quite bring myself to do it. I did wonder, though, why Jack had been at this shopping center.

Was he on a case? A stakeout? Maybe involved in some high-stakes, international, super-secret job?

His life was so much cooler than mine.

I glanced at the businesses that occupied the complex with Cady Faye Catering—a dry cleaners, a real estate office, a dentist, a scrapbooking store, a gift shop, a nail place, and a restaurant specializing in vegetarian tacos. I preferred to think that a totally hot private detective wouldn't shop at any of those places, but I guess even Jack Bishop needed to get his teeth cleaned or his shirts pressed.

I cruised past the stores and the large display window that had "Cady Faye Catering" printed on it in large white letters. I'd been inside their shop on my first visit here a few weeks ago and knew there were comfortable seating areas, books with photos taken at previous Cady Faye catered events, all set in tasteful décor befitting their upscale clientele.

Cady Faye Catering had built a great reputation over the past few years and had asked to be added to the L.A. Affairs' list of approved vendors. None of the other planners had wanted to take a chance on them. L.A. Affairs lived or died by its reputation so none of the planners wanted to make a mistake—and possibly lose their job—by giving something as important as the selection of the caterer to a company no one had worked with before.

I'd learned about Cady Faye—owned and operated by two sisters, Cady Wills and Faye Delaney—a few months ago when I'd stopped by my parents' house as the caterers were setting up for one of Mom's dinner parties. My mom was a former pageant queen—really—who thought she was still a pageant queen, so no way would she cook for her own party. She'd never complained about Cady Faye's food or service—and believe me, if Mom hadn't liked anything about them she'd have said so multiple times—which assured me they'd done a great job.

I'd gone to Priscilla, the office manager at L.A. Affairs, and told her I'd like to give Cady Faye a try. Priscilla had given me raised eyebrows and a slow headshake, but I'd persisted. The more Priscilla had resisted, the more I'd wanted to use them—which I prefer to think of as my generous spirit not the mile-wide stubborn streak some people have mentioned, as if it were a personality flaw. Priscilla had finally given in and agreed to let me use them, but I'd gotten a this-better-work-out grimace from her.

I could have tried out Cady Faye Catering on a small, simple event, but I'd gone with something bigger—a St. Patrick's Day party being given by Xander and Nadine Brannock, a young, up and coming Hollywood couple. I'd figured that at a rip-roaring St. Pat's bash I could see how Cady Faye operated—plus hardly any of the guests would be sober enough the next day to remember if the food had been bad.

I circled to the back of the shopping center and parked at the rear entrance alongside two of Cady Faye's delivery vans. Nearby were a truck unloading bread and a van from Maisie's Costume Shop, as well as a couple dozen other vehicles. Another catering delivery van was backed up to the open double doors. Cady Faye was expanding so construction work was underway on both sides of their shop. I grabbed my portfolio and squeezed past the delivery van into their small receiving area.

Inside, a line of workers in white smocks and hairnets carried boxes and trays to the van, preparing to head out for a luncheon somewhere, apparently. A dozen or so guys and girls—servers, I figured, since they looked like college students—milled around, some wearing a Cady Faye Catering uniform, others in street clothes. Construction workers hauled around equipment. The place smelled like sawdust and fresh baked bread.

I spotted Faye Delaney right away. She was an average looking late-thirties gal with sensible hair and comfortable shoes. She was talking to a leprechaun—or, at least, a young woman in a leprechaun costume. Neither of them looked happy.

As I walked closer I heard Faye say, "I don't know why she can't get here on time. Especially today. She knows full well that—"

"Oh, hi," the leprechaun said to me, cutting Faye off.

Faye spotted me and instantly morphed into everything's-great mode.

"Haley, so good to see you," she said, smiling broadly. She gestured to the leprechaun beside her. "This is Jeri Sutton, one of my hardest working employees. She's trying on the costume for the Brannock party for me. What do you think?"

The costume was beyond cool—green vest, bow tie, and jacket over a white shirt, green below-the-knee pants, green and white stripped knee socks, and black buckle shoes. Jeri looked great in it. She was a couple of years younger than me, tall with brown hair. She'd probably look great in anything.

"Maisie's Costume Shop is here fitting the servers," Faye said, and managed a brave smile. "On top of everything else that's going on."

I glanced around at the hustle and bustle that bordered on chaos.

"But it's nothing we can't handle," Faye said.

"I'll go look for Cady," Jeri said. "Somebody said they thought they saw her here a few minutes ago."

"Thank you, Jeri," Faye said, and exhaled heavily. "But don't be gone too long. I need you to model that costume with a skirt."

Jeri moved away and Faye said to me, "She's one of my trusted agents. I don't know what I'd do without her. She's in culinary school, you know."

I didn't, but Faye kept talking before I could say anything.

"Let me show you our newest toy." She talked as we walked, telling me about upcoming events.

The place was a bit of a maze, since they'd taken over the stores on each side of their original shop. Construction workers, the catering staff and servers were coming and going as we passed storage rooms, the huge kitchen, a cool room, and a utility room and janitor's closet.

Faye stopped at the entrance to one of the rooms and gestured grandly.

"The ice room," she announced. "We're the first catering company in the area to have one."

I walked inside and, honestly, it didn't look like much. Bare walls, a concrete floor, harsh overhead lighting, several chest freezers, and some sort of hoist. There was a big open water tank sitting atop a metal frame about eight feet off the floor with steps leading up to it and hoses sprouting from it.

I guess Faye picked up on my where's-the-ice expression because she said, "It's for making ice sculptures."

"I thought they were cut out of big blocks of ice with a chain saw," I said.

"They can be, but look." Faye opened a big metal door across the room. Inside was a huge walk-in freezer and shelves lined with dozens of ice sculptures ranging in size from a few inches to several feet—green four-leaf clovers, stars, leprechauns, rainbows, and just about everything else Irish you could think of.

"Cool," I said. "These will look great at the party."

"We can make them for any occasion," Faye said. "Let me tell you how it's done."

She closed the freezer door and launched into an explanation of how colored water was mixed in the big tank, then pumped into rubber molds and lowered into chest freezers by a hoist, and then everything turned into blah-blah-blah and I drifted off.

That happens a lot.

Edie, Priscilla, and whatever the heck was going on back at L.A. Affairs popped into my head. I wondered if I could find a way to stay out of the office for the rest of the day. Maybe tomorrow, too. I mean, jeez, if I wasn't there they couldn't fire me, right?

Faye jarred me back to reality by walking away. I followed, pulled the door closed, and we headed toward what I thought was the front of building—my sense of direction isn't the greatest—where the display room and offices were located.

We stopped at the entrance to the employee lounge. Inside were tables and chairs, vending machines, a fridge and microwave. On one wall was a bulletin board pinned with announcements, and on another ran a row of lockers; duffel bags and backpacks were piled up under them.

Near the restrooms, two clothing racks held leprechaun costumes. Guy servers rotated in and out trying them on, while the girls sat idle at the tables. I'd worked with Maisie's Costume Shop on other events and knew they'd do a great job.

Maisie, a stout woman in her forties who owned the shop, checked the fit on each server as they came out of the restroom, and her assistant Wendy entered their sizes on her iPad.

"Hey, Haley," Wendy called.

Like most of the wardrobe people I'd met, Wendy had a fashion-forward sense of style that bordered on outrageous. Today she had on boots, tights, shorts, a tank, and vest in progressive shades of purple. But since she probably didn't weigh a hundred pounds on a rainy day, she really pulled it off.

Faye's cell phone rang. She stepped away and answered it.

"Awesome costumes," I said.

Wendy gestured toward the clothing racks. "We brought skirts for the girls. Jeri is going to try on one so we can see how it looks. What do you think?"

"I think it will be great," I said, "as long as the servers don't look better than the guests."

Wendy laughed, then stopped as Fay's voice rose.

"She didn't get back to you?" she said into her phone. "She assured me she would. I'm so sorry. I'll get on it right away. Yes, of course. You have my word."

Faye snapped her phone closed and exclaimed, "Has anyone seen Cady?"

"Wasn't she here just a minute ago?" someone asked.

"I thought I saw her car out front when I came in," one of the girls said.

"Well, is she here, or not?" Faye asked, looking more annoyed by the second. "And where is Jeri? She's supposed to try on the skirt with her costume. Why aren't people here, where they're supposed to be? Things have to get done."

"I'll look for them," one of the girls said.

"Me, too," another one added.

"All of you," Faye said, "please, look for them. And tell them to report back to me immediately."

Faye blew out a big breath as the girls hurried out of the room, then caught sight of me standing nearby.

"Oh, Haley," she said. "Please don't think this sort of thing happens often. Really, we're all dedicated to the success of this business. I'm sure Cady is here somewhere and she's anxious to go over the menu with you."

"No problem," I said.

I thought there definitely was a problem but this didn't seem like the time to say so.

"I'll look for them, too," I said.

Honestly, I didn't know how I'd have any better luck finding

Cady and Jeri than anyone else, but it seemed like a great excuse to get away and call Kayla at the office to see if there'd been any new developments.

I walked along the hallways amid the hustle and bustle of the people who were doing actual work, and called Kayla's cell phone. Her voicemail picked up so I left a message. I tried the office line. Her voicemail picked up there, too.

Yikes! Did that mean Kayla was in with Edie and Priscilla getting fired? Of course, if that happened, it might be safe for me to go back to the office.

I mean that in the nicest way, of course.

I tucked my cell phone into my handbag and strolled along, trying to look as if I intended to actually accomplish something. It did seem weird that both Cady and Jeri were nowhere to be found. Maybe they'd both slipped out to a nearby Starbucks---I'd done that myself a time or two during the workday.

I opened doors along the hallway and peered inside. One was a storage closet containing plates, glasses, bowls and cups. Nobody there. The next door was linen storage; plenty of tablecloths and napkins but no people. The one after that was the ice room. I pulled the door open and looked inside. No one there either, except—

Something was strange about the room. I heard water dripping.

I got a weird feeling

Water pooled on the floor under the big tank. I hadn't noticed that when I was in here earlier.

My weird feeling got weirder.

I looked up and saw a black shoe sticking out of the water tank. Yikes!

I raced up the stairs. Facedown in the water was a leprechaun. Dead.

* * *

The paperback and ebook editions of *Duffel Bags and Drownings*, along with all the other novels in the Haley Randolph mystery series, are available on Amazon, Barnes & Noble, and your favorite online bookstore.

Made in United States
North Haven, CT
20 September 2023

41783944R00081